LOQUELA

ALSO BY
CARLOS LABBÉ

Navidad & Matanza

CARLOS LABBÉ

Translated from the Spanish by Will Vanderhyden

LOQUELA

OPEN LETTER
LITERARY TRANSLATIONS FROM THE UNIVERSITY OF ROCHESTER

Copyright © 2009 by Carlos Labbé and Editorial Periférica
Translation copyright © 2015 by Will Vanderhyden

First edition, 2015
All rights reserved

Library of Congress Cataloging-in-Publication Data: Available.
ISBN-13: 978-1-940953-24-3 / ISBN-10: 1-940953-25-0

This project is supported in part by an award
from the National Endowment for the Arts.

ART WORKS.
arts.gov

Printed on acid-free paper in the United States of America.

Text set in Dante, a mid-20th-century book typeface designed by Giovanni Mardersteig.
The original type was cut by Charles Malin.

Design by N. J. Furl

Open Letter is the University of Rochester's nonprofit, literary translation press:
Lattimore Hall 411, Box 270082, Rochester, NY 14627

www.openletterbooks.org

*For Mónica Ríos and
the Labbé Jorqueras*

Many tears at mass and many after. All of them like the passing day, and with all the pleasure of the internal loqüela, an assimilation or remembrance of the loqüela or music of the heavens, expanding devotion and affection with the tears of feeling I apprehended divinitus.

—Ignatius de Loyola

Loquela is a word that designates the flux of language through which the subject tirelessly rehashes the effects of a wound or the consequences of an action: an emphatic form of the lover's discourse.

—Roland Barthes

LOQUELA

THE NOVEL

Carlos closed the small notebook and the movement knocked the pen off his writing desk. Anxiously he yanked off his T-shirt and threw it into a corner. He was sweating. He got up from his chair and sat down on the floor. For a few seconds, he glanced through some photos from his cousin's party that were spread out across the rug. He opened the window and looked out onto the street. An organ grinder inspected the contents of his can, hoping for a coin. Carlos looked at his notebook and reread the last page: anticipating that the killer—whoever it was—would defend himself, the man had retrieved the gun. His head pounded and his knees were shaking. There's a dead girl lying inside, he thought. He'd never fired a gun. His vision clouded over, his whole body pulsed as the door opened slowly from inside. He decided to fire first. And he did. The albino girl let out a soft cry and fell at his feet. He was the killer.

This was not the ending Carlos had planned. But as he was writing it, he'd lost sight of the pages delineating the plot structure. It's like a weight's been lifted, he said to himself. Like escaping the body. Guided by the pen, in a sort of feverish state, he'd turned the man into the killer; and now the carefully constructed plot was a complete mess. His own ineptitude infuriated him: four months figuring out a way for the stalker to remain unseen while simultaneously leaving behind clear indications of his intentions; innumerable nights of the man following the albino girl, up all night reading chapters from the detective story she'd scrawled in that notebook. The man's interpretations of the woman's story, the walks tracing those absurd maps she'd invented, and the characters with names that obviously concealed the identities of other people. The staged shootout. Or, to put it another way, the strange coincidence of a shootout between cops and bank robbers and the chapter dedicated to bullets, on a parallel day at a parallel location, a warning sign compelling him to take up his own investigation. All of it so the man arrived at the right address, opened the right door, and shot the albino girl, the albino girl he wanted so badly. This final image was incomplete: after the shot, the man's eyes wouldn't come to rest on her body, instead, through the door into the next room, they'd find a mirror hanging on the opposing wall, and there he'd catch a glimpse of his own face, sirens drawing ever nearer. Even though he had ignored the novel's outline, Carlos thought, it was possible that this was his favorite part. He went to the kitchen and opened the refrigerator. He brought a jar of red juice to his lips and drank, asking himself how the letter the protagonist sent to the wrong address had led to him being followed by an unknown car, to a death threat in the bathroom of a dance club where he'd gone to look for the girl one Saturday night, and had suddenly found himself embroiled in a shootout in the middle of the street. He remembered his friend's comment when he'd received a popular detective novel for Christmas the previous year, that these kinds of books were more machination and less mystery all the time. They've got no soul, Elisa would've added. She suggested the possibility that the plot of his book was the result of a sick imagination—that of the protagonist perhaps—and that the only recognizable thing in those pages was the presence of an albino girl doomed to die. Every time she offered an opinion about what he wrote, his girlfriend claimed that his characters weren't human beings. They never yawned, they didn't shower in the morning, and never woke up in a bad mood; she'd say: the author should keep in mind that during the day he had to use the bathroom, laugh every now and then, and sleep a little after lunch. This would prevent his characters from forgetting their own bodies every time they jumped, or ran, or shot somebody.

Carlos looked out the window again and saw the organ grinder walking away, his instrument on his back. A little girl was pulling her dog's leash, trying to get it to stop barking at the poor old man. There were no bullets out there, no persecutions, no deaths, he thought. Of course, the organ grinder was afraid that the dog might bite him, or that someone might assault him while passing through certain neighborhoods. He tried to remember being in a similar situation: the novel's protagonist felt fear, seeing his own deformed reflection on that wall, gun in hand, the face of a killer. He picked the pen up off the floor. He'd been mistaken, he said to himself, as he sat back down at the desk: he didn't want to write a detective novel; he wanted to write a mystery.

He'd decided to take a break from the novel, he told Elisa. They were lying together on his bed. His notebook was still open on the desk, the uncapped pen, the jar with what remained of the powdered juice. She was staring at a white canvas that hung on one wall, her back to her boyfriend, who was holding her. I need to take a step back from the plot so I can figure out who the characters are, he said; you'll finally find out whether they're flesh and bone or paper, she murmured. You were right, he added. That it'd be good to get to know the man, find someone who looks like the albino girl, talk to both of them. Elisa closed her eyes and took hold of Carlos's elusive hand. They lay there in silence. From a neighbor's house they heard the shouts of children playing. She looks like Violeta, Elisa said. Who?, he asked; the albino, the albino girl looks like your cousin's friend whose name is Violeta, but Carlos had never seen her. Elisa got up, went out into the living room, and came back to the bed, holding a photograph between her fingers. She sat down next to Carlos and pointed out a figure dancing on the edge of the dance floor, near some tables. The girl was albino.

It was the final meeting of his detective fiction class. Carlos sat down in the back, near the aisle. The professor was trying to summarize what they'd covered that semester in a long monologue, replete with authors but lacking quotes or plotlines. The closed windows and door made the room's air unbreathable; Carlos's head began to nod with sleepiness. None of the students he knew were in attendance; there were only four people in that class, which was the last one of the semester. All of a sudden a hand touched him on the shoulder. Carlos jumped, surprised. Without completely waking up, he turned to see who it was and found the rows behind him empty. A pair of eyes backed away from the door, eyes belonging to a face he barely recognized and that he'd forget immediately. He stood up abruptly, bumped into a desk, someone timidly told him to be quiet. There was no one in the hallway. He went to the bathroom, splashed water on his face, and went back into the classroom just as the professor was talking about the error of making light of death, the state from which the story you tell is always a mystery.

Elisa opened the door to Carlos's house with her copy of the key. Relieved, she found that her sketch was still on the table in the middle of the living room. As she was leaving, a letter that had been slipped under the door caught her attention. She looked for the mailman on the street but saw no one. Just seeing the name of the sender made her want to get out of there, but not before putting the envelope in her handbag. On the corner she ran into Alicia, Carlos's cousin and housemate, and they talked about the weather while she racked her brain over and over, wondering if at some point she and her boyfriend had been together with Violeta, the girl who'd written the letter.

Carlos's mother came into the bedroom and opened the curtains to wake him up. She told him he shouldn't sleep so late and that she was on her way to the store. Putting on makeup in the bathroom, she asked him if he'd be staying for breakfast. Either way, he should stick around until she got back, because his father was at the office and Josefita shouldn't be left alone.

Carlos got in the shower. Massaging shampoo into his scalp, he remembered a forgotten chapter that was saved on his parent's computer: the protagonist is supposed to meet the albino girl at the ticket counter of a movie theater, but she stands him up. He heard the engine of his mother's car fade away in the distance, and the insistent ringing of the telephone. Dressed now, he peeked into the living room and greeted Jose, who was talking to a friend on the phone, but she didn't respond, as if she hadn't seen him. He sat down in front of the computer to review the chapter and print it out. He'd never asked himself why the albino girl didn't show up for the date. The protagonist, on the other hand, had an immediate hypothesis: she'd been kidnapped; the stalker had found her at last. There was no doubt, her message had indicated that particular theater, not another: the stalker had doubtlessly run into her randomly on some downtown street, let's say the corner of Ahumada and Moneda, where people always sit and stare at the passersby as if searching for someone, and all because he'd insisted that they meet. Near the mouth of the metro he rested, fatigued, on one of the benches; he didn't see anyone suspicious. He realized, looking at a clock on top of a post, that it was earlier than he'd thought. So, he said to himself, one of these people could be the one who abducted the albino girl; that old man flipping through the headlines of the afternoon paper, the kid eating French fries, the guy with the shopping bags and the sweaty face. But none of them fit the profile he imagined for the maniac, they weren't suspicious faces; in fact, they were intimidated by his scrutinizing eyes, right then the clock on the corner read two minutes past seven. He went back to the theater—worried that the albino girl might already have come and decided to leave, disappointed that he wasn't there—in vain: they weren't going to meet that night, and he decided to go in and watch the movie. Fucking public clocks, you never know if they're broken or on time.

His mother's voice interrupted him. She was coming up the stairs, asking with feigned calm where Josefita was. In the living room watching TV, he suggested. His mother searched the house, top to bottom, calling to Josefita over and over, but the girl had disappeared. She was too old to be hiding, but not old enough to go out on a walk or to run off with a friend. None of the neighbors had seen her leave. When his mother came up to the second floor for the third time, swearing, asking him where Jose was, Carlos felt the weight of a hand on his shoulder again, like someone was watching him from the doorway. His little sister had been taken while he, lost in thought, read a chapter on the computer screen. He ran through the neighborhood's surrounding blocks, but like always, the streets were nearly deserted. A nanny was monitoring some children in the plaza, a nurse was pushing an old man in a wheelchair, and a few dogs were sniffing around on a corner. In which of these tranquil apartments could Josefita be? How was it possible that she'd not overheard a single worried conversation, a single knock, a single shout? When he got home, his mother was waiting for him, smiling: his father had called while he was out to see if he should pick something up for lunch, and she'd told him desperately that Josefa was missing. His father had laughed, because more than an hour before, he'd come by to take her clothes shopping. He'd even parked, come inside, used the bathroom, yelled to Carlos that he was going out with Josefina and, without waiting for a response, they'd left.

Kneeling on her bed, Elisa studied the name of the letter's sender. It'd be so easy to open the envelope and read the words Violeta had written for Carlos. But she'd never do it: opening that letter that didn't belong to her might unleash the strange person who over the years she'd managed to hide away in the cardboard box that now sat open on the floor, its interior revealing folded, yellow papers, old notebook pages on which Carlos had written poems and letters that he'd given her in the most sentimental days of high school. Elisa threw Violeta's envelope into the box. Then she replaced the lid and concealed the box in the very back of her closet, near the ceiling, next to a moth-eaten superhero costume and a pink sleeping bag that only came up to her hip now. She closed her eyes and lay down. It was more like she was recalling a significant dream than really falling asleep: fade to black; Carlos's eyes finding hers the first time they saw each other, in an elevator in the apartment building of a mutual friend. The heat of his shoulder when she'd cried at a party. And him not daring to touch her. His voice had been different, so serious, when they walked home together, always following the same route. She'd loved him in high school. Loved him like that, young, pretending to be tormented and solitary but surrounded by a large group of friends. She adored the game of randomly running into him on any one of the ten corners that separated their houses just to make him think about the two of them. They never touched each other, that was the promise; he gave her obscure poems and she gave him looks, nothing more, but all that ambiguity got old, they couldn't go through life guessing, so the mystery got boring, she confused him at parties with other guys, she didn't want to be alone. They trivialized one another, Carlos would've said at the time; they became best friends, confidants. Elisa knew that he liked to lie, that he was lazy. He teased her for taking half-hour showers, for competing with every girl she encountered, and for acting like she didn't know she was beautiful. On the phone, once a week and once a month face-to-face, that was their agreement. They discussed the minutia of their lives over beer, then they'd walk to her house in silence, nostalgic for something that had not yet happened.

One day Carlos called her and asked if she'd have any trouble getting a formal dress. She said no, she'd even put on some makeup. He'd decided to go to his cousin's wedding and he wanted her to be his date. They danced with each other, they had a good time. They talked about marriage after a few too many drinks. She swore that she'd never get married, he said he'd heard it a hundred times before, that love isn't eternal. They stared at each other. Remembering that night, Elisa always used whiskey to justify what they did. But this time she limited herself to remembering that they'd climbed the stairs holding hands, gone into a dark bathroom, and that one of them had locked the door. He asked her to kiss him, she made him promise something, that they'd stop talking, that they'd stop being themselves, and the mouth that agreed was a strange mouth, whose penetrating smell and unknown moistures lasted until the next day, and when the sun came up they were no longer best friends. They kissed again to open their eyes and studied the details of each other's features. He said something clever, they laughed and started talking again. But Elisa had never forgotten the stranger from that wedding night. She covered her face again, a large mouth sucked at her until she started losing air not realizing that it was her own breathing.

Violeta's letter, in lines not written for Elisa, might be intended for that intruder—the one who'd bent her over the old bathtub in that unfamiliar bathroom and stripped off her clothes—for that man who appeared when she was sleeping and heard noises, bells, moans that she was sure were coming from the closet, from the box she'd hidden behind all of her clothes.

THE RECIPIENT

I'm so tired. I woke up with the sensation of having not slept at all, of having traveled thousands of miles during the night. And in the mirror, my face wasn't great either: two puffy circles around my eyes ordered me back to bed, but I was already standing, I had to go to class. The images from my dream would've kept me from shutting my eyes again anyway. I took a shower.

I dreamed, like I never do, all night. If I wanted, I could enumerate all the stages of this exhausting dream, this long and vivid dream. I know that Alicia, making fun of everything as usual, accompanied me to a room in my old and unfamiliar country house in Rancagua, that she played dolls with my little sisters (affecting voices, inventing frivolous plots: Barbie goes to the salon and some strange stuffed elves give her a new hairdo while gossiping about other toys, laughing at a headless Playmobil); that she slept in the same room as me, in another bed or in a sleeping bag on the floor, like a childhood sleepover: we turned off the light and talked for a while, but fell asleep in the middle of an important conversation (maybe just when I asked her who she liked, whether or not I was the one she loved?). Another time she went to school with me, we skipped class and went to talk on the far side of the playground. I didn't know it, but she was following every move I made and every word I said, in the afternoon she showed me a garish comic strip she'd drawn that featured me. A synopsis of my day in vignettes, something like that. I never got bored of her, nor she of me: the same old story. Then suddenly, Alicia disappears.

I'm in a corridor in the big house that belonged to my uncle. Near Coya, down a busy, unpaved road, any local can tell you the way if you ask. A fantasy house, immense and silent, accessed through an electronic gate, a fountain and gravel parking area appear. (Being very young, I didn't get why they covered the ground with sharp little rocks, particularly when we ran barefoot across it on our way to swim in the pool.) A fantasy house, as I said, that often appears in my nightmares along with that other house, the wood cabin on the shore of some southern beach where I've never been, an invention where J liked to predict that she and I would someday live.

I found myself in my uncle's house, sitting on the parquet of a long corridor, that echoing corridor where, when we stayed overnight, the great thrill was to jump out at someone at the last second without them noticing your approach in the darkness. And the silence of that house. It still disconcerts me every time I see (or better, admire) the four people who live in that place, forced to live with the knowledge that, day after day, there's no one lying in any of the beds in any of the ten or twelve bedrooms, that the soap in all seven of the bathrooms remains unused, the showers clean, but rusty. The emptiness in that house becomes unbearable, and so the birthdays and Christmases that my family celebrates there are competitive displays of affection and camaraderie, to fill the silence between conversations. And, because there's something terrifying about letting them trail off, the conversations become banal, then personal, repetitive, uncomfortable, then banal again, an uncle, an aunt, a great aunt, and another uncle think they've been talking to me, but we just make sounds with our mouths and we keep on like that, not hearing one another, until they get in their car and go back to Santiago in silence, immediately turning on the radio—music always saves us from that horrible muteness. (Why can't we sit quietly and look at each other? Why do I get nervous when Alicia says nothing, when I ask her "what's wrong" and she pauses before responding, "nothing, I just don't want to talk"?) Music or the newspaper or a book, never just the two of us.

I was sitting in that corridor with some of my cousins, but they weren't actually my cousins, they were old friends from high school; insulting each other jokingly, making fun of the each other's foibles and defects for a laugh—they're the same even in a dream. We were obviously children, dressed in bathing trunks and playing a game of some kind across the rectangles of the parquet. Marbles, or something. And while, bursting with laughter, we were competing to say the cruelest joke, someone steals the bag of marbles from M, he bites R's hand, R starts crying, C mimics his cries, M screams "abuse" in falsetto, I watch poor R earnestly, we all start slapping each other, repeating the worst jokes. I made some suggestion, N insulted me, I was tripped, and I fell down. Everyone jumped on top of me in a little pile, and it would have been futile to use the air that was scarcely reaching my lungs to scream that they were suffocating me, that I was dying, because just as I was starting to feel desperate, the human tower fell to the ground. Then, as we were getting to our feet and M was picking up his marbles, a grownup came over (an adult, I remember someone whispering "sshh, a grownup is coming," heavy black shoes resounding through the house), and told us, calm down, you little shits. The grownup continued into my uncle's bedroom, the master bedroom. I left the group of kids and followed him down the long red carpet in that twilight corridor, wine-colored walls barely illuminated by the small dark bulbs of the few hanging lamps. The grownup turned back to me, a finger placed vertically across his lips, commanding my silence. I grew along the way, it was now extremely difficult to see the details of his big shoes, and when he turned and told me to be quiet I saw that he didn't have a face. Terror.

Alone, I went into the bedroom, decorated and furnished in identical fashion to my uncle's actual bedroom. An enormous television, piles of photos, a table with flowers, pastel curtains tied with olive-colored cloth ties, empty nightstands on each side of the immense master bed. An unnerving piece of furniture with locked drawers (there are secrets here). The warm sun and the fragrance of pollen and fresh cut grass coming in through a window that opened onto the garden—spring in Rancagua. A young girl was sleeping peacefully.

I wanted to get out of there; I hate disrupting other people's sleep, especially when it's someone I don't know. But the door was locked. I looked around the room and sat down on the bed, at the girl's feet. Her back was to me, her body wrapped in the sheets. Softly, I touched her, she didn't wake up. I think I said something.

I prodded her, nothing happened. Little by little, I became more forceful, until I found myself with my hands on her shoulders, rolling her towards me, shaking her. She was very pretty, apart from her dead eyes. Dead eyes and cold skin. Her mouth: clenched so tightly that her teeth had ground together before she died. I'd never seen a corpse, but knew I had one in front of me now. (Her white hair—a noteworthy detail—resembled the nylon wig of a doll.) Repulsed, I let go of her and ran to the door, which was open.

Before leaving the room and waking myself up, I looked at the girl one last time to see if her eyes had recovered their glow, if her pale skin ran with blood again. The angle of her arm lost its rigidity, she became human, and with revived fingers, uncovered herself. She stood, her voice so unexpected said thanks, many thanks, and who might I be, a new cousin perhaps. "But," she went on, "haven't they told you that if I'm made to remember that person whom I hate, the loathing I feel is so strong that it paralyzes me, that it kills me? No, I'd already forgotten that person, but when I saw the trunk full of papers, I was overcome with rage. And why not? I'm going to die on the floor of my house, snarling like a rabid dog!" (And with her eyes she indicated the trunk, a trunk just like one that had belonged to my grandmother, heavy, ancient, and cold because it's made of metal.) "His disgusting body is in there. I opened it and found him. I wanted to kill him again, cousin, a hundred times. Before he killed me." (But what she told me is impossible; a body would never fit in that trunk.) Then my eyes fell upon the trunk and, slowly, it began to expand, transforming into a coffin. (Or was it maybe I who shrank, turned back into child?)

Then I woke up and went to the bathroom. Then to the kitchen, still half asleep, and I realized that someone had slipped a letter under the door, a letter that got the recipient's address wrong. The sender's name is "Violeta Drago." Do I know her? Of course I know her. She's the friend Alicia has been crying over, locked away in her room all these days. The friend who was apparently murdered in her own apartment, a horrible crime that was never publicized. Just now, I remembered a time when Alicia showed me a video from her graduation, she paused the video to point out her friend Violeta, the albino girl.

◆

August 12th
12:13

I write little because I'm beginning to value silence. During break Alicia and I discussed the uselessness of writing just a character's initials, it no longer drew attention to the connotations of the names, the characters lost immediacy and simply became letters (she's reading Kafka). I'm tortured by hundreds of images and ideas, I can't maintain coherence in my diary. So much to say, but also so much noise: cars, footsteps in the hallway, the telephone . . .

It was Alicia calling. Why does her ability to silently absorb the problems of others attract me this way? Why does being next to her physically paralyze me? Why, over the phone, were we functional (functional? we're not machines)? I'm sad and alone in the middle of a sad city. Alicia seems better prepared than I for the constant aggression of Santiago's inhabitants; she seems to always be going somewhere. (Once, awkwardly, I asked her—she was on the verge of tears and I didn't know if I should say something, which is what her friend who died would've done—what she did for fun, and she said, "I never wanted to be here, that's why I leave sometimes.") Alicia, never serious, told me during break that if I wrote a diary or something like that, I should name her A and not Alicia, because readers would invariably associate her with that little girl who went to Wonderland, a situation that was not at all accurate in her case. I am sad, a delicious wind is blowing, the myrrh trees are already in bloom.

Yesterday afternoon T confessed to me that he was starting to scare himself. Every year, at the beginning of spring, he experienced a sensation of overwhelming emotional catastrophe. "Like the driver of a car who discovers that he's dead a second before crashing," he said, hearing the birds start to sing, the blue sky, the warmth returning. Then he confessed to me: couples will start making out right in front of my eyes, walking around holding each other, happy, and I'll be alone. Winter coats and summer orgies won't do; spring speaks the truth: some come to this world alone and others come in groups. (T asks for advice, I maintain my position and invent experiences to support my words. Then I hate myself: but I can't stop lying. I'm not sure anyone would be interested in what I'd have to say if I could.)

(According to Blanchot, Sade says the only way to avoid suffering is to enjoy the giving and receiving of pain. But, at the same time, the only way to transcend the vice of sadism is to become unfeeling, because vice makes me weak again, rendering me dependent on pleasure and pain.) If only for a little while I might stop feeling. (Although I think that is impossible in this harsh, biting world. In the city of Santiago, pausing in the middle of the street, when the face of a girl demands your attention, bears as

consequence a car blasting you with its horn, a woman gestur-
ing "get moving, jackass," a delinquent selling ice cream stepping
on your feet in the rush to board the *micro*. And by then the face
would already be lost in the swarming crosswalk at Lyon and
Providencia.) To write is to feel myself dangerous in the moment
I do not hesitate. But I must accept that in a diary I'm allowed to
be obscene. (I think about J, her small face between my hands, "it
hurts," "you make me feel like a slut," then I kiss her forcefully.
Awful night, her really awful bed, the worst part is that it was I
who was there. And afterward I fled, what a coward. J, forgive
me. Yes, I do feel bad.)

Alicia loaned me a magazine from Uruguay. I'm staring at a
photograph of Pizarnik, the article says that she realized with horror that writing was keeping her alive, and the result of this was
her spine-tingling poems. In her face you can see how greatly she
needed the silence. "A great writer of letters," says the caption.
What is this lush mystery in the correspondence of strangers?
Why is it that I'd kill to gain access to the stack of letters that
Alicia says is her prize possession? (I want to be honest, I aspire
to that in these pages: I've been waiting several months for two
letters: the one Alicia sent me from Czechoslovakia last summer,
marvelously trivial, without a doubt, but something of her, for
me, indelible smile would arrive in that envelope; the letter that J
implied she was going to send me, if I'm not mistaken, telling me
off over and over, after describing in cruel detail what happened
that February night when I was a monster. The postal service took
care of losing them, and I've not heard from J since. And what if
Alicia finally did decide to write me, is it possible that I'll never
get to possess her handwriting?)

And yet, the letter from Alicia's friend is still in the drawer. It's taken an effort not to open it, I should give it to Alicia tomorrow, it's addressed to her. (Every time Alicia sat down next to me in the quad, she seemed to be searching for a word. I talk and I talk. She remains distant. Is it possible that Alicia was born while her parents were traveling abroad somewhere? No, that was her friend, the one who died, the one who spent her life thinking of a way to escape, "to go back," as Alicia says. Back where? And I chose to hide myself in this dusty apartment instead of wandering through the deserted fields of Rancagua.) They say that Alicia writes too, poems maybe. Pizarnik's eyes. Pizarnik's mouth. The professor at the university, with the uncomprehending smile: "Poetry is the woman: an image that contains and expresses itself through suggestion, with silences; narrative is like men: another image, but this time expansive, overwhelmingly explicit and verbose." But Alicia looks so sure of herself, she gives me a sidelong glance and tells me about things that happened in her childhood. When she names them, the ten people she's been involved with in her life, they revolve around me, as if I knew them.

◆

August 12th
7:50 P.M.

I don't want to sit and write, I'm exhausted, but if I stop I'll forget myself. I took an hour-long nap, an hour and a half, give or take, and I dreamed. This last week the nightmares have been constant, the face of the albino girl (Violeta?) cupped in the hands of some man. The man caresses her, she maintains a stoical expression of sensual pleasure, a face of false enjoyment. The man was me, I mean, it wasn't me but the resemblance was horrifying. It was Carlos. The phone woke me, a telemarketer or something; I realized that it'd been years since I'd last written about Carlos and his girlfriend. At that time, J lived only a few blocks away, we'd wait for each other in the square, for the other to appear when one of us was sad and needed a shoulder to cry on. (And this longing, what is it?) I would give her little sheets of paper with poems written on them. Wow.

Pathetic Carlos. I found the notebook containing the story I wrote the summer of my and J's first kiss. "Carlos is actually just the opposite of me, I'm a coward. He's fearless, he acts," that's how the opening paragraph starts. I took out Violeta's letter before lying down to go to bed. I stared at it. What would Carlos do in this situation? Open the envelope and read what it says.

◆

August 13th

Wasted day. I've slept and slept, just now turning on the three lights in my room and the radio to wake myself up. I've never thought of dying by my own volition, but today I came close.

I feel like puking. I have to go to the bathroom every fifteen minutes and my face is burning. I drank a lot last night; this morning, walking to the university, an old lady offered me a job selling chocolates in an artisanal market, probably because I reeked horribly of alcohol. Self-pity is the word. Alicia used it against me and I couldn't keep the tears from falling. She stopped the car and sat motionless, looking straight ahead, like she was still driving. Understand that I was drunk, that I've forgotten almost all my words and instead remember every single one of hers: they hurt as if they were burying me underground. I know I talked to her, or tried to talk, about the almost inexpressible pain the thing with J caused me. In her face I saw disappointment, that she was bewildered by my tears, that she was thinking: "So that's the big mystery, a simple case of loneliness and the inability to be alone."

"I'm trembling. Delirious." That, according to Alicia, was one of her dead friend's favorite expressions. Yes, I believe that justice should exist, that yes, there's such a thing as kindness. And then I realize mistakenly that these are just verbal constructions, because I can't help but think that last night I got exactly what I deserved: a few months ago, in a car parked along the curb, I was the same worn out statue that Alicia was last night. And J qualifying her miserable life (that same lack of self-love) was just like me, sitting in the passenger seat, watching my own tears fall. Without knowing it, Alicia hurt me the same way I wanted to hurt J when I told her I never wanted to see her again, never again. I wouldn't be surprised if Alicia told me the same thing last night. The symmetry, which had already disappeared, makes me think about God again. That I was a religious being, or something like that, added the callous Alicia with a reproachful tone. I should see a specialist; "check yourself in," she told me. And me in the morning, almost having to force myself to get up: I'm bound for madness.

I called Alicia, the maid told me to hang on. She came back, unfortunately Alicita just went out, I wasn't able to catch her.

(White lie?) I don't want to lose her, I don't want to forget her faraway look, her rigid posture in front of the steering wheel; last night she was a wise woman. She'd never been as attractive as in the moment when she revealed her deepest disdain for me, and at the same time, deep down, she wanted to help me see beyond the pit where I've stuck my head. I'm going to puke.

I don't want to write about myself anymore, but it's no use, TV and music don't work; books even less; not the phone either. I just received a telephonic greeting from a supermarket; after hanging up I had to fight the urge to dial J's number. I miss her, but I wouldn't be able to handle hearing her. Alicia is so decent: she told me she didn't want to know anything about J, it was what it was, not a single miserable detail of the sordidness that went down between us. Alicia and I. Me and J. Like that time in the country, when my dog tore half of the chickens to shreds. My mom was horrified and I decided to teach him a lesson: I started by kicking him repeatedly over in the corner of the chicken coop until the poor thing cowered, howling in pain. I kept hitting him even though he looked at me with his most pained eyes—I was the master and I was giving him a beating. I restrained myself when he dropped to the ground. Then I ran to the river. Sitting on a large rock beside the brown water of a rushing branch of the Cachapoal, I watched as my dog approached, his head bowed in pure shame. He came up to me, frightened and guilty; I petted him. He was ashamed, even though it was I who'd almost beaten him to death, taking advantage of my superiority! What would Carlos have done? He would've taken each dead chicken, put it in front of the dog's nose, and then slapped the nose quickly and deftly. He would've seen Alicia, rigid in her seat, approached her and, gently turning her head with his hand, kissed her softly, just lips, the way J kissed me in the car to force me to make a decision: truly damage her or be her friend again. And I waited for her to say the words: "Okay already, if that's what you need to hear: do whatever you want to me." But instead, I started the car, drove her home, and told her that we'd never, ever see each other again. I don't know if I said goodbye to Alicia last night. I would've given her a kiss just like Carlos, like the other guys who stayed in her car, oh how I wanted her, but how can I imagine leaning in, how can I forget that what I'm writing isn't my diary but the diary of another, which in turn forms part of a detective novel or a study of death. (Thinking it over carefully, Carlos wouldn't commit the blunder of kissing his cousin. Because Carlos and Alicia are first cousins: two individuals of such rare will can only be bound by blood. He's had a girlfriend for several years; yes, he wouldn't dare cheat on Elisa, especially with his cousin.) I need to get my head out of this pit; I'm going to turn on the TV.

(Edgardo Marín, the soccer commentator, says he's not surprised at all that a player punched a reporter, that an ex-soldier gave an uppercut to a student protesting about disappeared detainees, and not only that, but it didn't surprise him that everyone acted like nothing happened, like it was perfectly normal for Colo Colo's owner to force a reporter to leave a press conference and for his colleagues to just stand there, regarding him impassively, not even getting up and leaving in solidarity. Because [he says, and he's right] if I get used to living in fear, the frustration makes me a monster: fear engenders violence. I tried to rape the girl I loved, the next day the whole thing was silenced, it never happened; or worse, she and I decided to stop seeing each other, to stop talking, but the more it's hidden the deeper the wound gets, until I can't take it anymore and I get up, go to her house, and force myself on her, tearing her clothes amid her desperate screams and my pleasure, would I really feel pleasure? I live [we live in Chile, the commentator says] with a head full of filth. That's why I'm going crazy, I can only write dreams and alcoholic deliriums, unleashing the monster [the other]: I'm Carlos's scattered dust. And that's why Alicia stared straight ahead while I burst into tears in the car, because she's not from here, she has nothing to do with these dead bodies [the ones that'll inhabit these pages], because she's kind, even though she denies it, even though later, her jaw set, she says: "you don't know me at all." As always, I'm simplifying, I'm idealizing, I'm very literal; I should run away to the country that Alicia's from, to the city where her friend Violeta wanted to live. Or where she is now. Here in Santiago we're all going to end up stabbing each other.)

◆

August 16th

A quote from a different magazine: "Kristeva changes the location of things. She always destroys our last prejudice, the one you thought you could be reassured by, could take pride in (Barthes)." I should go back to reading. I wish I had more desire to write, but I'm exhausted. Abuse of the pen, the hope or the struggle to make this diary form part of something greater, so that it illuminates and is illuminated by another text. On the other hand, there is the fear that I've forgotten the important moments. (What is a diary if not a retelling, an attempt to give narrative significance to a life that has no order? A deception.)

Saturday night, during a party at S's house, Alicia completely ignored me, and I couldn't get into the game. We were strangers for hours, like I didn't know she was following me with her eyes. At one point we found ourselves dancing face to face, and our movements seemed to correspond to two entirely different songs, then she disappeared toward the kitchen. A while later, I ran into her again: I was dancing enthusiastically and laughing with M; she was letting P wrap his arms around her. (Fear of the future, when she'll be off traveling and not here.) She wasn't the same either, struggling to show me that I wasn't just another random guy on the university quad. She barely smiled, she didn't ask how I was, even though she always does. (There's no one else like her, I say, but I prove myself wrong if I go out on Providencia and count how many girls there are who're just like J.) Before getting up off the bench in the quad (she's always going somewhere), Alicia asks me to stop talking about the party: "Who are you, the one from Saturday or the one from Thursday?" I respond that today I am Carlos. She doesn't laugh. I'm losing my spark, she said this herself. With a distinct quiver of her tight lips, Alicia tells me that tomorrow she is going to give me something, something I have to read as if it were more important than any of my unspoken obsessions, dedicate more time to it than to my thesis. I kiss my thumb and say: "a matter of life and death." (She blinks, she hates me, I don't want her to go, I want to spend my last days with Alicia.) She doesn't find my comment funny and stands up.

◆

I've decided that, for the moment, I've said enough. I should read, read, otherwise my own writing will become repetitive. Just like Alicia or J when you spend too much time with them: words begin to become excessive. All that's left are the gestures, the looks, the hands, the mouth.

I have a large envelope containing two notebooks that belong to the albino girl, Violeta. Belonged, I should say, she was writing in them just before she was killed. One of the notebooks is green, the other is covered in wrapping paper. One of them contains paragraphs she calls "Descriptions of the Sea"; the other, her dreams. Alicia gave me the envelope so that, in exchange, I'd give her the letter from Violeta that was (mistakenly) delivered to my address. I must read, read.

(A little drunk, Alicia asked me who this Carlos was that I'd been talking about. I told her that I'd send her another letter that would endeavor to explain this inexplicable thing. She told me that I'm evil. In spite of myself, I came up with a sentence from the intolerable *La nueva novela* by the homonymous Carlos Fuentes, regarding Cortázar, Oliveira, and Traveler: "Confronting the double incarnation there are only two answers: murder or madness." I think about how fond J and I were of *Hopscotch* at one time, just like Alicia, who told me that when she was sixteen she did a sort of pilgrimage through the streets of Paris where the drama of Oliveira and Maga unfolded, I don't want to laugh at such innocence. Talita and Maga, Oliveira and Traveler. The problem with doubles is that they must inevitably exterminate each other. At some point I'll write about Goytisolo's *State of Siege*, where he claims that everyone has a virtual enemy. Who am I going to kill if I'm my own enemy! The only part of *Hopscotch* that's worth the effort is the part that takes place in Buenos Aires. The final schizophrenia.)

◆

August 18ᵗʰ

In the dining hall at the university I kept repeating the phrase "this is not a good year" and P got pissed off, she almost threw her food in my face. During my thesis seminar, while the professor was talking, making sterile attempts to provoke some sort of response from us students, I observed the faces of my colleagues: heads down, eyes inert, hands hidden. Smug mouths: we've already heard this too many times, this is interesting but it's too early in the morning and the sky is very gray; what the professor was saying was external, we're in our final year of studying literature and in one way or another we've made up our minds to forget that we don't want to be here. The book was actually entertaining, like TV, parties, the cinema. The photocopies had a distinct smell, we can simulate an analysis of the mythical structure of *One Hundred Years of Solitude*, for two hours we drink down lessons of generative linguistics with our coffee, the rest of the day we live! We walk around the campus, holding hands with our girlfriends, we go to a theater performance, then suddenly a book appears in the display case. One book. We touch it, it's a beautiful edition. I sit down in the plaza and run my eyes over every line, every letter, I enter that historical world, I'm just another one of those characters on the edge of the abyss and my skin is crawling, I convince myself of repulsive human uncertainty, of suffering, of the declamation, of the verbal chaos, and of the silence of the last paragraph; ominous, death. I turn off the light above my head and think in silence: "If God doesn't exist then this is all there is: disappointment, depopulation, the asepsis of the word *end*." You don't think about the courage of writing a novel in a Santiago on the brink of collapse, it doesn't occur to you that the only valid thing would be to make up poems in your mind, like Borges, entire verses in your mind, go over them a couple times before falling asleep, and the possibility of their publication evaporates forever; you enjoy yourself for a while fantasizing about how publishers and critics should be executioners of benevolent smiles; you don't think, you just feel. You turn the last page, the image of the protagonists curled up together, cynical, afraid to pierce the moment with the word; the question "how are you, are you still sad?" actually means "I can't hold you any longer, we can't spend our lives holding each other, sheltered from the world"; which actually means that when you turn off the light above you, you discover that your body exists and functions on its own, that if at some point you're lucky enough to be sleeping with your wife breathing deeply a few centimeters away, you'll dream of another woman, in spite of this you must wake yourself up, slowly pull her close, and repeat that you love her, that you live together.

(Abuse of "that," the self-indulgences of my writing "that," the colon, and the semicolon. Proof that I write poorly but that I say something, always with the same words, yet saying something that matters. I reread this. My head hurts [abuse of "but"], but for the first time in many days I've been able to recover a passing happiness. I'm alone, I repeat to myself, and yet there are so many pages, so many names, so many years.) You lie down with a book clutched tightly in your hands. The book has done all of this to you: weeping. Real tears, really. Not like the ones that you shed during the drunken display in Alicia's car, the sea that ran down your face, rupturing the false desire that was growing between the two of you, too soon, too forced. I abuse repetitions, I lose plotlines. You wake up early, the faces stop screaming at you, that hand retracts from your body, the albino girl from the dream evaporates. You know that today it is an anxious Carlos. You do everything quickly; you don't sing or think about Alicia in the shower, no breakfast, the *micro* comes by on the hour and you find a seat next to the girl with the curly hair, the really attractive one who's always talking to people by the water fountain in the corner of the quad. You show up to your seminar, still tasting the novel, wanting to open up to the professor and tell him, with complete respect, that during the part when the guy and young girl have their encounter in the middle of the jungle (or was it in the middle of the dance floor dressed up as beggars or transvestites?), you got a phone call from Alicia. The funny thing, you'd tell the professor, is that, for a second, Alicia's voice was J's voice (it's possible, both voices are deep and delicate), which made you shiver; the book fell from your hands and the glass of red powdered juice that you were drinking slid off the table. The professor might smile at the anecdote because he's a good person, you know you're not that funny, you're already tired of playing the fool. So that's it, the professor's smile injects a soft warmth into your body, tomorrow will be less gray, the time not so early, the dream will have vanished. Even when the professor takes attendance, in the moment that he asks if anyone knows a certain individual who has never attended class and you suggest that perhaps it's a pseudonym, you think you hear a burst of laughter. The professor didn't get the joke, the other students keep staring at the floor with empty expressions though this time they're firmly griping their book bags, getting ready to leave as soon as possible. Someone laughs, but you see that there's no one left in the classroom. "Funny," you think absurdly, walking and promising yourself to try to write more entertaining paragraphs; I promise to find out what it is that's hidden in my books: the warm slap, the irresistible phrase with which Alicia wakes my eyes from their lethargy.

THE NOVEL

Sitting on a bench in the plaza, Carlos was drawing a tree. He groaned and crumpled up the paper, realizing that every day his lines were getting worse; the tree he was sketching looked nothing like the one in front of him, it was more like a building or a statue. A few days ago, his little sister had asked him to teach her to draw hands. To start with he showed her how to copy her own, the left. But in the end, Josefa looked at his drawing and narrowed her eyes: that's not a hand, she said, it's the claws of a beast. He put the sketch down beside him and looked around the plaza. A modest, pretty schoolgirl passed by in front of him. Holding her by the hand was a man dressed in a suit and tie, one of those guys who'd run you over to get to the bank on time. What a waste, thought Carlos.

Then he picked up his sketch again. He didn't give the couple another thought, they'll end up on some bench somewhere, as usual, he said to himself. The tree was no longer a tree but a gathering of strange shadows, immense stains suggesting shapes: a couple through a window and perhaps someone spying from the corner, lying in wait. He was distracted by a cry that gradually became a scream: a girl was calling for help. He walked calmly to the other side of the plaza, where he found a circle of onlookers gathering around the same schoolgirl he'd seen before, whose torn uniform didn't cover the bruises on her legs. A compassionate woman who was trying to console the girl retrieved her buttonless blouse from the bushes. A man was asking questions. The degenerate had run away, he realized, and the schoolgirl cried, ignoring all the people, hands covering her face. Nothing about her was sexy now, just the opposite, he thought, walking away. He realized that the girl's blue uniform was just like the one Elisa had been wearing only a few years before. He remembered afternoons junior year when he'd wait for her outside the school before they'd walk home together down Alcántara. Sometimes she walked a few steps ahead, other times he led the way, but walking backwards, facing Elisa. He never took his eyes off her, not her, not that uniform; he could barely contain the desire to slip his hand up under her blue skirt. He called her from a payphone, fearing she wouldn't be there. She answered and asked him a question: why did his voice sound so different, like he was someone else entirely.

THE SENDER

At last. If it's difficult for you to comprehend my writing and you get lost in my inconclusive sentences it's because I write against the waning day. My hours are like cups of water confronting a thirst. Although I'm trying to be as honest as I can, understand that not even on the edge of the pit can I find a way to say the right thing. What matters is my ultimate sincerity, that which speaks to the other, to you and not to me. I'll use up a lot of ink adapting to your presence, but I trust that it'll be worth it, or better, that I did the only thing left for me to do. Because there's not one disinterested sentence here, not even being crazy about you, as they say, alters my intention: to tell you why I found myself forced to abandon Neutria.

When I was a little girl, my hair came down to my waist and sparkled like the snow. Fearful, that's how children are. But once, hearing Alicia's warning cries, I turned around and there you were, concealing the scissors in your woolen fingers. I snatched them away from you easily, while you looked at me with surprise but without fear, the same look—let's say empty yet impassioned—that you gave me last Saturday at Alicia's party as night was falling; you were intoxicated and charming, and I was intrigued when you responded that yes, that now, with me, you were someone else and not Carlos in Neutria. Let's not go quite so fast, just fast enough to unsettle your reading and to make you aware that your Sunday headache isn't just the result of a night of drinking, but of having remembered the most important and hardest thing to remember.

Back then I was very small. You know: smiling, secluded inside the house, my long white hair seeking the light of day to shine. The girl kept hidden three houses away from yours. I spend my time playing with Alicia, tall and attractive. You boys tease us, calling us Snowflake, Miss Transparent, Glassgirl. My hair, long as a summer day, is an obsession for you, because you enjoy ruining things that require care: you stomp on flowers in the garden of a woman who lives all alone, you wake up early to rearrange the pages of the newspaper, freshly dropped on the doorstep, you terrorize, with a dozen different calls, your neighbor's cage of parrots. You threaten me: doll hair, we're gonna cut off your doll hair. I've gotten used to seeing you through the window, brandishing scissors. I don't even tell on you, I just run to my room. Alicia is the one who confronts you, with her deafening, high-pitched screams, one time I punch your most annoying friend, the fat one, in the face, and he goes off and cries behind a tree. You make fun of him, and for a little while I get you guys to forget about my hair, because you're busy inventing a supposed romance between Alicia and her victim, the fat boy.

Allow me this speed with which I write you, a different rhythm from the immobile sentences I sought in most of my notebooks; it's just that, inevitably, there's someone zeroing in on this house, someone who wants my end. I shouldn't say this, but what I hope is that you stop him. Besides, at this point in my recollections, you should already be able to guess what comes next. Because another year passes and again one of you begins to fixate on my hair, which I spend my time brushing. The end of summer, an unusually detailed image from early childhood: the city grayer than ever, people running over each other in the streets to buy textbooks, pens, spiral notebooks, even the sun's presence is lost, dissolving into the monotone sky, dirty, more dust than anything. It's the awful Santiago of our childhood, doubly abandoned. So bad that I only recall one moment of fun that took place outside the confines of the house: two naïve girls shouting gleefully, soaking each other with a hose, white with green stripes, me and Alicia. All of a sudden, she freezes. I see myself turning instinctively around and I find your eyes, wide with surprise. You hide the scissors behind your back. I come at you with a violence that frightens even me, grab the scissors away from you, your friends, hanging back a little ways, speculate in low voices, expecting you to defend yourself, not just stand there, impassive, not crying or smiling, doing nothing: that's a difficult expression for a child to make. Serious as an animal. We leave you there, fixed to that spot, and go inside the house.

You should know this part better than I do. To me it seems that what happens next is that in the following days your group of men—forgive me, boys—gathers in the rundown shack at the abandoned train station that you guys call The Clubhouse and they decide to make an example of you, or maybe to kick you out for being worthless and a coward. The truth is that after I take the scissors away from you, all the pranks you guys pull fail, and so the group begins to fall apart: one family leaves the neighborhood, others disappear without explanation, you avoid meetings at The Clubhouse. It's possible that you guys just got bored of each other or were too busy with school. I remember realizing that life in the passageway was ending and that we were entering Neutria when I watched the other boys stop in front of your house on their bikes and invite you to go get ice cream; you come out and don't know how to lie, you don't understand why, but they believe you when you tell them that you have to go to the supermarket with your mother, for the first time you're able to get out of going with them, and you're left alone in the exact moment that Alicia and I say to ourselves that from now on this is Neutria, without even knowing what we mean. I know, I can already hear your arrogant response: it was a childish way to give name to the unknown, to evade fear through familiarization. That's what you said to me on Saturday, at the party. That sometimes, when you thought about it, you found our overflowing imagination interesting, an intriguing subject for a novel even; but a few pages later we were tragic, demented, frightening.

What comes next is the moment in which my childhood multiplies into details I'd love to recount and cannot. Most of them were lost the instant we played together, the rest are still there, in Neutria, and you can see them for yourself. Sometimes Neutria was the land of semi-divine emperors, of infinite cruelty or kindness, whose slothful and obese courtiers, in contrast, engaged in decadent melodramas. Other times it was a simple village where farmers, shepherds, and foreigners traded honey, cheese, bread, or fruit for a song or an entertaining story. Or it was the nexus of activity for stylized spies, convertibles, casinos, firearms, hotels, highways, and femme fatales. And in the middle of all those adult faces appears a boyish one, yours, insistently inquiring what it is that we're playing, and coldly I reply that we're playing the city of Neutria, not expecting you to make fun of us: you talk to yourself—my mother says people who talk to themselves are lunatics. Alicia gets up, says again that it isn't make-believe, that Neutria exists; it's a beautiful place, incredible, we travel there on long weekends with our parents. It's so much fun that we like to recall everything that happened there. That's what we're doing, remembering all the wondrous things, not inventing them.

Of course, you're the only boy who talks to us and asks us questions. Alicia and I don't talk about this, but we're fascinated that you come around and bother us. Make memory, that's what I said to you, with oh so drunken words, at the party when you came up and hugged me and asked me how I still remembered: you were my first, one never forgets her first. It also pleases us that you watch us play through the window and then ring the doorbell and run away, because there's cruelty in our inventiveness, because your doubt challenged us. The game changes. The two of us go on to describe everything that occurs in Neutria in order—I start writing in notebooks, we draw a rudimentary map—and from one day to the next every detail of Santiago interests us: the drainage system, the hierarchy of the authorities, the traffic, the demographic distribution, and I surprise myself by paying great attention in my history and geography classes. With the sole objective of convincing you of Neutria's existence, I open my eyes to the place where I live and realize how much I hate it, I also hear how much other people abhor this chunk of concrete and how much they'd give to move to the coast, to the beach, to the cordillera, wherever. Yes, I know: this is nothing new.

It all began as a joke, as a small act of vengeance, because you had doubted us, and so it was only right that, in the end, it was back in your hands. Remember that winter, the last one on our street. You knock on my door every Friday afternoon and sarcastically ask us why our parents weren't taking us to Neutria that weekend. Forgive me, what you say is: that strange city. Alicia and I are sitting by the fireplace, that first time we're eating a big chocolate bar with almonds, and that is your excuse for coming in. It's raining, of this I'm certain. Alicia says we can't go to Neutria, it's dangerous to cross the great suspension bridge that leads to the city in a storm. The Black River is treacherous, it swells violently, swallowing cars and the boats coming in from the sea, rumor has it that it feeds on them, seriously, but also that this is the river's way of protesting that monstrosity of a bridge that's been built across it. You listen in silence, probably imagining the river not as a swollen stream but as an aquatic animal with a hard, aquamarine hide, something like a shadow. Then you ask if it eats people too, or just cars and boats, a silly notion, but we try hard to take it seriously. I hurry to respond, citing the legends of Neutrian fishermen, and then Alicia quickly recounts in specific detail the story of a man who, after falling in the river and being rescued, claimed to have been saved by a marine monster. You listen with amazement to the story that Alicia invents on the spot, with total disregard for the rules of Neutria we spent every afternoon writing. I felt betrayed, for the first time I hated her: I was jealous of the attention you were giving her. That night we argued, yelling at each other. Alicia didn't understand why I was so upset, for her it was all in fun, we were just making fun of you, of how much you wanted to meddle in our business. I calmed down when she proposed that we come up with a new way to humiliate you, using the stories that you asked us to tell. Remembering how you sat down to listen to us, open-mouthed, sometimes asking absurd questions, making us feel superior, clever, intelligent, special, because you were foolish enough to believe us.

Until one day you stopped coming. The next day we waited for you, and the day after that, but you had disappeared. I didn't tell Alicia this, but I was miserable all week, I thought you'd gotten bored of our stories about Neutria. Not telling them made me forget about that city, it gave me the horrifying sensation that I was trapped in putrid Santiago. If I'd known what was coming, I would've preferred your appendicitis got worse rather than have you lie to us. But you lied and our laughter came to an end. On Sunday, you showed up unexpectedly and we went out onto the patio and asked you what'd happened and you stood very still, looking us in the eyes without blinking. You said: I went on a trip with my parents, they took me to visit Neutria. Alicia and I were only quiet for a second, we had to say something or we'd start to cry. It was the end of the game, a situation we'd foreseen so many times, the point when—according to our plan—we'd burst into savage, irrepressible laughter; choking, we'd tell you that Neutria didn't exist, and how could someone be idiotic enough to try and make us believe our own lie. I was about to say something but Alicia beat me to it, and it was a disaster: my neighbor, my playmate, my best friend turned on me. She sat down next to you, took your hand, smiled at you, happy because at last you knew Neutria. She asked you questions about the redesign of the Plaza de Armas, whether or not you'd gone to the ice cream shop near the entrance to the black beach, if by chance you found the board-walk pretty. The words were already beginning to sound faraway, I couldn't stand to be in that place any longer, that place I didn't love, that place I hated. That afternoon was one of the last times I saw you, before the party last Saturday night. And yet Alicia and I have stayed in touch. It's been hard for us to go back to being the friends we were when we were young, but there were a few summers when she did come see me in Neutria.

THE NOVEL

Carlos read each paragraph and then, emitting a soft tsk of his tongue, tore out the page. He'd been doing this for quite a while: he stared at the alarm clock on the nightstand; it was two in the afternoon. He was still wearing pajamas. The same confusion persisted that he'd felt when, upon waking, opening his eyes, and contemplating the ceiling, he'd run through in his mind the day that awaited him: revise the novel, write the missing parts, a final pass with a lead pencil or red pen, like a professor hurrying to correct his students' exams. He hated having to visit those faraway albino girls again and again, to fire the fateful weapon that hurt no one, like he was writing a screenplay for a cartoon. He'd rather stay in bed, trying to recover the thread of what he'd dreamed in the middle of the night. He still retained a few images: an infinite castle that he couldn't look away from, because his head was the only part of his body not buried in sand. And the epilogue, if he could call it that, when he came to a pleasant town where the sea's freshness made him feel weightless. He went into a barbershop—not a stylist, nothing like that—and the barber, wearing the face of a childhood friend, greeted him with a joke. The door opened, a woman appeared whom he didn't recognize, but who he knew to be his girlfriend because she hugged him, whispering that this was the way she was going to bring him back from the dead. And she kissed him.

He recalled something the professor of his detective fiction class had said: death should not be taken lightly. Repeating this advice to himself, he went to his desk and took out the notebook that contained the novel. He read quickly: it was a holiday the day the man learned of the existence of the albino girl, that she was in danger, and that she'd come searching for him anyway. The streets were empty, so it was easy to watch her cross over, eyes fixed on him, paying no attention to the car approaching at full speed from the opposite direction.

He had the impression that there was nothing alive in this notebook. He asked himself if at some point this page—meticulously concocted with twists and turns and more twists and turns—might form part of a book, whether this machine of actions would cease. And he tore it out. He read the next one and the next. Always the same, fifty pages of chasing after a woman who reveals no clear reasons for why she's being pursued. It was already two in the afternoon. He paused, reading over the ending: the protagonist didn't react when a man shoved him. He left the bathroom, convinced he should confront the fat man behind the bar. He'd ask for a drink. And when the guy came over he'd warn him to stop playing games, he'd been found out. Stop calling the albino girl, no more men following her home or threatening him in the bathroom while he was washing his hands, he'd say, his voice grave. He made his way through the multitude that was moving euphorically to the sounds of a popular song. Suddenly the lights came down, a rush of couples holding hands descended on the dance floor. The protagonist was climbing the stairway to the second level when he stopped: on the dance floor, in a corner, he recognized the confident stride and preoccupied face of the albino girl. He stumbled his way back down, losing her for a second in the crowd; he had a hunch he'd find her near the exit. He grabbed her arm and asked her what she was doing there. The girl—blonde hair, straight back, tight dress—looked

at him uncomprehendingly: it was someone else. He apologized, embar-
rassed by his mistake. Back on the stairs a bouncer blocked his assent;
the police were clearing everyone out, something unfortunate had gone
down between the fat bartender and a drunk with a broken glass. The
bartender defended himself, they fought, there were blows, and the one
stabbed the other. Carlos stopped reading. He thought that the protago-
nist, shaken by the coincidence, should've marveled at his luck, but he
didn't. Instead he shoved the bouncer who was describing the situation
out of his way and went up to see with his own eyes what had happened,
and ended up getting kicked out. The error was that his characters never
noticed what was right in front of them and were instead always trying
to see past it.

He stared at the pile of torn-out pages sitting on his desk. He became
aware of the connection between that particular chapter and a phone call
from Elisa that'd woken him up one Friday at six in the morning a few
months ago. Her voice hesitated when she told him that she'd gone out
dancing with her friends that night, after drinking all afternoon and
reminiscing about existential discussions they'd had in high school. That
night, at the club, they ran into one of her ex-boyfriends, and before long
he and Elisa were conversing in close proximity, then he convinced her
to dance. Just when she said yes, Elisa spotted him, Carlos, leaning on
the bar, staring out across the dance floor. She shuddered and went over
to him, but it turned out to be some random guy who tried to wrap his
arms around her, proud of having seduced her with a single look. That
morning Elisa, drunk, asked his forgiveness over the phone. She also told
him that she was sure he'd appeared there in that instant to look out for
her, to make sure she didn't do something stupid.

The sound of the door being unlocked distracted Carlos and he got up
and went to see who it was. Elisa walked in slowly, carrying heavy bags

that she set down on the floor; she came over and kissed him. She made fun of the pajamas he was still wearing. Seeing the torn-out pages on the desk, she didn't bother asking what had happened, she just went into the other room to find a box of paper clips. One by one she began putting the pages back into the notebook, trying to follow the order of the story, but Carlos grabbed her from behind and began to lightly bite the nape of her neck until she gave him her attention.

THE RECIPIENT

August 18th

Blanchot again, but read this time in Librería Gradiva, near my apartment, so I'll cite it from memory: to write "I am alone" is comical, a farce, because the simple fact of writing it refutes it. The paper, the reader who reads the phrase, the proofreader, the publishing house, the publisher's propaganda, newspapers, the translation, a citation in a foreign text, then another and another and on and on until it grows commonplace and gets used in some magazine, on TV, in everyday conversation, and, in the end, it loses all meaning. Hundreds of people accompany me when I write that I am alone: writing is a renunciation of solitude. No one writes to read themselves, no intimate diary is private. And so I impersonate my voice in these pages (but of all the voices, which one is mine?) to make them resemble an article by Fernando Pérez about Adolfo Couve that I read in the magazine *Vértebra*. The honesty those two taught me, which I love to resort to, compels me to transcribe the first footnote from that article: "The text is composed by alternating fragments from my diary (often transformed, tightened up, corrected) with my observations and outside citations inserted into the text a posteriori [. . .] as a kind of counterpoint, to compensate for potential excesses of subjectivity." In these pages, I've copied the form in which Pérez approaches his analysis of Couve's work; and yet I'd forgotten this model for my voice until this afternoon, when I found the magazine in question among my photocopies. (I should just write, I'll delete all the "I"s from the sentences later, I'll remove the allusions to easily identifiable individuals, I'll erase the overly personal fragments, I'll make corrections to avoid problems, no big deal. I should take a moment to laugh at myself for having pointed out the problem of solitude, for checking to see if someone is sitting down beside me to read what I'm writing, for noticing the inevitable curiosity that overcomes you confronting a page covered in the handwriting of someone you know.)

I go back to reading Violeta's notebooks, without any value judgment at this point. I had an erotic dream about her; it wasn't entirely her, but it was an albino girl. In the morning, Alicia and I are sitting in adjacent seats. She looks around with a peculiar expression that I don't recognize, I wonder if I might have something to do with that look, if it's true that it seemed to call me phony, phony Carlos. She leans back against the wall and for a few seconds her thin shoulder rests against my arm. Call me a fool, but I wanted for the day to stop passing, for that boring class where our surfaces touched not to end. But that night, with a kind of bitterness, I couldn't tell if it was a put-on or not, she said: I want the Carlos from last week, I don't want you. (But how is it possible that I'm a substitute for the Carlos she knew if she is the only person I've told [as far as I remember] about what's afflicting me? It must be that what's actually happening isn't easy to describe, the proof being that I'm still unable to slip a single certainty into this notebook.)

That afternoon I talked to my mom on the phone. It's cold in Rancagua. My grandmother is suffering from migraines and the doctors can't figure out what's wrong with her: it's not her blood pressure, not her medication, not changes in temperature. They say she's really lonely. (And if during her birthday party they were to make the whole family be quiet so she could get up from her armchair—where she'd been sitting motionless all afternoon, acting like she wasn't there—and say: "My children, I have to tell you, without beating around the bush, that loneliness is making me ill," what would my father, my uncles, my cousins do? Who—out of all of us who feel alone [all of us?]—would leave their life behind to be with her? Without a doubt none of us would take her words seriously. Without a doubt none of this would ever happen: my grandmother asks for a general silence only to thank God for giving her a family like this one.)

I'm heading down Providencia chewing over the episode that I just finished reading in one of the notebooks, where, at a party, Violeta suffered her first delirium. I focus on the fact that the word "delirium" seems to be written by someone else, a different handwriting superimposed over the old title, which has been erased. I hope I get to talk to Alicia about these adulterations. "No one else has seen these pages," she said when she gave them to me. Could it have been her? I need to wash my mind with soap. I see the eyes of the people walking at Providencia and Pedro de Valdivia, I focus on their faces. I head home on Once de Septiembre, I pretend to ask about some CDs in a store but the employee's response annoys me: I've never seen the people of Santiago more absent than today. No one is talking, no one is watching where they're going. A gringa sings Madonna at full volume while listening to her headphones. I'm surprised to hear an organic sound in the middle of the intersection of Holanda and Providencia. The gringa, spooked, shies away from the look I give her and quickens her pace, no doubt I'm a psychopath, a clown, or another gringo. I cut perpendicularly across the sidewalk to disrupt the flow of pedestrians: a man with a briefcase, an old lady with a shopping bag, two students smoking themselves to death, another executive with a ringing cell phone. Nobody runs into me, they avoid me with the skill of the occupied, I'm just another obstacle, another post en route to the office. My mediocre experiment fails. Disgusted, I get ready to throw up my arms and scream at full volume: doesn't anybody have anything to scream in this city! But I don't do it, I just keep walking, in silence, like always.

◆

August 23rd

Who shot Violeta Drago? I should write this question down, I should ask it every time I read one of her pages. The truth is that there's no answer. That's why I keep taking notes. This morning I wasn't able to say anything to Alicia, now hidden away in the library, when we were talking about whatever insignificant thing (is it possible for a conversation to simply be banal or is it oblique, am I really short-sighted enough to believe that her comments are actually about the latest album by whomever, or about the Canadian film we saw on Friday?). When it comes to talking about reality, the subject has never been us, it's always been the unwanted miscue that forces us to opt for impersonal dialogues. When I ask her about her weekend she invents some story so that I'll leave her in peace: her friend found himself, in the middle of the dance floor, bored with the seventies disco music; he said he was going to the bathroom, but what he did was go get in his car and leave her stranded at the party. I don't know how to react to this anecdote, I look at her and she looks me right in the eyes before she says okay, I'm going, and turns around and walks resignedly away. The moment for saying things is yet to come.

The important thing is that a few hours later, contemplating the rain (today it has rained magnificently), I randomly run into Alicia again. When she sees me, her expression is transparent. For an instant my face must be identical to hers. Of course, we conceal ourselves again, taking refuge in neutral terrain, a lame joke from me (and you, I thought you'd left), a sudden presence next to us. (The friends, the third parties, who appear out of focus in every movie, who in realist books are barely named, who in day-to-day life can become omnipresent and harsh in their judgments, like the comment L made today after Alicia left, that who would've imagined, back in our first year, that I'd be such good friends with the girl in the black dress and combat boots, irony or no. Maybe it's me who has yet to understand egoism and who pays attention to irrelevant voices, voices that, for the sake of mental health, one should only listen to the way one listens to car horns when crossing the street.)

And I haven't felt weak again.

Right now, in this moment, despondency pulls me to my feet. I know that today's words are more repetitive than ever and my pen weighs a ton. I've read too much over the last few days, I transgressed on Friday when I asked Alicia if Violeta was mentally ill. With glassy eyes and an unanticipated seriousness in her voice she said: "Jackass. And I thought that you—" She went to the bathroom, and I acted like the guy who's acting like nothing's going on, but without a doubt I'd blunderingly ruined the morning. My comments (they lost any novelty a long time ago) weren't going to get me anywhere, and wearing the same face as always wouldn't either. The rest of the day was filled with evasive, failed attempts to bridge the gap with a phrase, and too much time, and a fucking silence that (I believe) festered in me alone.

That afternoon I read, mistrustfully, Violeta's chaotic recollection of her father, of the moment when he brings her from Neutria to Santiago. The trip lasts an entire night and the girl calls on absurd resources to return to that cynical paradise that she baptized as Neutria. (On Saturday, at my grandmother's house, I carefully scanned a political map: where Violeta would've located her city of origin, there's nothing—miles of coastline, not even a fisherman's cove. I mistrust geography, traced as abstractly as Violeta's, yet imposed by years of pretense and a cadre of shysters who've agreed to turn the horizon into lines, dots, and limits.) I fantasize about an investigation, about a trip Alicia and I might take in the summer to search for Neutria. We'd use the albino girl's diary as a kind of guide, along with a roadmap composed of all geographic versions of Chile—colonial cartography, military maps, trip plans sold in gas stations, international guidebooks for gringo backpackers. Then I get tired of speculation: Neutria might, or not, be a city with a semi-hidden physical existence, as Violeta claims. But is it possible in this day and age for a town to really be inaccessible? (Clueless. You trust information in such a visceral way. Something to do with your attachment to books, your disastrous habit of enjoying the TV newsman, your pathetic solidarity with the words people say.)

Enthused, I asked the professor a question and kept my eyes on C while listening to the answer. Sitting beside me, she returned my look and told me that this boring major wasn't worth studying anymore. For some reason, her comment made all my enthusiasm vanish and the class itself turned gray, monothematic. In the middle of the classroom, surrounded by my classmates, the loneliness was palpable. As if it were a game, and I were the only one who wanted to play. As if I were somewhere else, far away, in a sunny city by the sea where the literature that's taught isn't a collection of themes, of structures, of forced characters, but is instead the part of us that we're unable to see. I saw myself following Violeta to her city, sitting down in a classroom at the university she attended without permission to listen to how the professor and the students conducted their discussion—some of them standing, some bewildered by the succession of interpretations—between the outbursts of lachrymose laughter from one student who'd had the world that he'd read in some novel or other destroyed by the professor. A student was speaking with a hesitant voice but in the first person, quoting with precision and gesticulating, as if the coherence of his sentences might call into question the validity of his existence. When the professor looked directly at Violeta and said "don't you think?" she could no longer stay silent, she got up from her seat and went out into the hallway.

I seemed to be there, and yet all the other seats were occupied by my actual classmates, dead-eyed, discussing whether to change the date of a quiz or the due date of an assignment. Apathetic, slumped in their chairs, seeming not to hear or see, but I applauded when Violeta left the classroom, and watched as the kid with the expressive hands went after her and—she described it this way herself—grabbed her arm, asking her name and what year she was. V didn't pay him any mind, find out for yourself, she said, she came to these classes because she got a kick out of the ridiculous enthusiasm for literature; occasionally it was a good spectacle, when it wasn't she'd go to the beach and take a nap. What I'm saying is that all of this came to an end when (my question in the middle of class) C confessed that she was sick of studying Literature at Universidad Católica. It's sad.

I've been reading nonstop. Coincidences disturb me and stimulate me and give me faith (my pretentiousness is unbearable today). The question mark of Neutria, my doubt is illuminated the minute I start doing research for my thesis on Onetti. The Uruguayan invented a metropolis, Santa María, inspired by Faulkner. (García Márquez did too, but I ignored him.) I should read more Onetti, not just out of academic responsibility. (But why does the existence of Neutria matter to me, why does it matter if Violeta wrote a novel or a chronicle? Onetti himself has ceased to exist; I don't recall seeing his face in any photo, I don't know anything about his life except that he died. Onetti could have easily been the pseudonym, the heteronym, the alias of another writer; the literary identity of a journalist working in Santa María. No matter what, there will always be someone who empirically proves the impossible. Without a doubt, right now a detective or a visiting judge is trying to clear up the actual facts of Violeta Drago's death: according to the file she was a maniac with pen and paper, but all paths inevitably lead to Neutria, to the fictional address, because in Santiago there's no evidence and no suspects.) Saturday I almost dialed Alicia's number to ask her about Violeta's city. Sooner or later she'll make me offer an opinion, a hypothesis about her friend's death, because clearly she didn't give me the notebooks for my own enjoyment. And here I am, seeing ulterior motives in Alicia. (But what's wrong with that? Carlos has always enjoyed detective novels.)

On Thursday afternoon I told C about my anxiety. I was lying in bed, worn out. I didn't want to see anybody I knew, the mere idea of picking up the phone made me want to puke. But I desperately needed to get out of my apartment and to speak. For a moment, I wished there were a place in Santiago where strangers could sit on benches and have conversations without having to interact in what we call social relations. A pretty little plaza with trees, streetlamps, and life. Where? Nowhere, dreaming, you knew it right away. As if La Cañada or La Alameda de las Delicias still existed, as if people still walked arm-in-arm, she said, as if we were of an age to go sit in the Plaza de Armas and watch the people go walking by. Then she told me about a place in Spain, Alicante, San Sebastián, like she was remembering it herself. A place where old people go to retire; there, facing the sea, they have set out hundreds of chairs, and when the weather is nice, they can sit down wherever they like to watch the waves come and go, to deliberately converse with anyone who is nearby. Imagine that in Chile such a place existed, a place called Neutria.

◆

Before entering my room I sense an odor, a foul, rancid odor. How is it possible? My own body disturbs me, I can't even begin to imagine the displeasure I provoke. Ah, please, forgive my indelicacy in these notes. As might be expected, I read and read all week long. I was hoping to give fate a chance, what chance! Look at me, reading the weekly horoscope—a habit I no doubt retain from afternoons spent with J—where it says that Thursday is a special day: love moves into the phase of compromise. Alicia is so far away, I cannot see her and yet I evoke her, even now. (Why don't I just use her initials like I do with everyone else, why does she have the luck of being the woman whom I name while writing this diary, the only one not victim of my lethal capriciousness?)

The horrible thing is that reading doesn't make me calm; I spent the afternoon thinking about Donoso, about *Coronation* and its protagonist who doesn't live life, but just reflects on it. (Do I want to be him?) I regret getting drunk so easily, just because C is celebrating her birthday, I am going to reject Alicia's invitation to dance. Too many questions await me back at my desk. Yesterday, coming back from playing soccer, E's friend's car turned a corner and, instead of asking them to drop me off, I let out an absurd laugh. A few blocks later, realizing we'd passed my address, they stopped. They asked me why I hadn't said anything, I said I didn't know.

I think about corruption, about indecency, and about the unfathomable. At C's party, J was dancing, talking, and laughing—happy. I know I didn't deserve—nor did she—an explanation (or even a greeting), but we were both waiting for one. That's why, in these first days of spring, I take up the contradiction of writing this diary, revelation and concealment, the resplendent whiteness of the page and the hope that if I play enough soccer, if I write and write, I'll be able to distance myself from the terror that after reading me, no one will ever want to see me. Give me shelter. I can't go on.

◆

August 27th
12:00 P.M.

I want to explain myself but I am not, I'm not capable. My head hurts, my vision is spinning, and I'm nauseated. I felt deranged reading what I wrote last night with the last of my strength, its meaning escapes me now and I don't understand why I repeat the same words over and over: my re-creation of Neutria has failed. I wanted to arrive at that city, using the same methods as Violeta; alcoholic excess took me elsewhere, somewhere far wetter and more fateful than paper. Now my body is paying for that compulsion, if I'm brave enough to sit down with a pen I'll explain later.

While I made the bed and vacuumed the hallway, I thought about F. Peréz's (or Roland Barthes's) explanatory sentences regarding his article on Couve: he doesn't structure the text as a daily diary for rhetorical authenticity, not at all, rather he does so out of a desire to construct a discourse with marks of the process by which it was written. I refuse to let myself agree, I write this way because I lack the indifference necessary to construct a narrative object that's alien to me, even if only in appearance. I admire this in Couve, Donoso, Balzac, Henry James, all those who, lashed by the storm, are able to cling to a third person, to produce dialogues without the intervention of the I, to describe, to divide themselves into chapters. As if in the middle of his suffering, in the moment they activated the electric chair, the condemned man ran through his mind a fairytale he'd composed in his cell, and he felt no pain, because his head was so occupied with finding the precise perspective from which to approach the final scene, when the protagonist finds the girl's body. ("I regret nothing" is the only thing that Violeta wrote, every day during the second half of July; the days of August were left blank, and then, furiously, she recounts a dream similar to one I had, if I'm able I'll write about it later.) Is that not, perhaps, what Violeta is doing, inventing a false city to escape from the days of Santiago, from the fact that there's someone stalking her with letters and phone calls, following her to class, perhaps not just one someone, but several? The doorbell is ringing.

◆

August 27ᵗʰ
7:56 P.M.

"Just like dogs, I experience that need for the infinite." Here in Santiago, nobody barks, and even if I heard barking I wouldn't be able to go see what was going on, who is biting what. I wish I were Lautréamont, I wish I could write just one sentence without paraphrasing, I wish I'd been born before the printing press, and that I didn't speak with someone else's voice whenever I want to make myself understood, to say what it is I imagine. (I'm going up to Alicia during a break, ready to blurt out what's eating me up inside: I love her. She looks at me stiffly, even though these days the spring air is sweet and lifts spirits, she doesn't smile at me. Just arcs her eyebrows. I open my mouth: "Like the dogs, I thirst for the infinite." Her surprise is barely visible. I don't get it, what're you trying to say. I don't know, I answer, quieter all the time. But that's the sentence.)

But no, I would not have liked growing up without a library in the house. Honestly I'd despise my own ignorance even more, I'd believe in the ability to know everything through reading, I'd be a fucking parody of an academic. What is Alicia reading? I only know what she told me this afternoon: a costume party, a movie, a book all afternoon, and alone. I turned back toward the window and for a moment she was plainly sad, the pain in her bright eyes, the unusual movement of her fingers is unwritable, just like J's hypocritical smile last night. Did I mention that I saw her—smaller than ever, a shy little girl—on the dance floor? She's not pretty anymore, her thin waist developed rickets, the neck I sometimes bite in one of my nightmares was a vulgar piece of flesh. (Frightening, today, my inability to hold the pen. I endure getting the shit kicked out of me, like in that dream when I stayed asleep, blood in my eyes, knees to my face, and yet I can't stay seated throughout the day without perspiring, without my eyes burning and my tongue turning into cloth. Much less read.) Cross off Friday, full moon falling and buried, total darkness, and that's how it should be, get used to it.

In last night's dream, Alicia opened her legs for me in a white room. J led me by the hand up the street toward Cerro Santa Lucía, we lay down on the dry grass; Alicia and I were naked, we couldn't keep from clawing each other's skin, I could barely breathe through her biting. I clung to both of them desperately, but neither of them was who they seemed to be: Alicia had that particular taste of cigarettes that belonged to J; J's smile verged on foolishness and malice, like Alicia's. I prefer to write it like this: confusion, amalgamation, I don't want either of them except in pieces. Alicia's ears, J's mouth, Alicia's hands, her eyes, J's chin and torso, Alicia's hair, again her eyes. The hours go by so fast and are so false, it's stupid to stay up late when I have a tower of books waiting for me. Dreams don't matter either, I dream on the surface and thousands of images pass me by without stopping, I don't laugh or cry, I recognize none of the faces that brush up against me. I wake with the certainty that I've been up for three days.

◆

August 30ᵗʰ

Physically exhausted and mentally ebullient. Absorbed. And I dream: again I find myself in the middle of a classroom at the university, all the desks are empty. Next to me a certain professor is waiting for the rest of the students to arrive, he gives me a friendly look and asks me questions: why do I think attendance is so low, are his lectures inadequate. As usual, I get ready to tell a half-truth, "you lack a certain profundity that approximates something literary, but we're not really capable of expecting much anyway." The scene is nothing more than a replica of everyday life; this is something that actually happens to me, I show up too early or move too slowly, such that, when I go to pick up J, I have to wait for her and converse with her father in the living room; or when I drop her off, we take so long saying goodbye that we wake up her little brother or run into her parents coming home from a dinner, a little drunk (them or me), and engage in these bizarre but fraught exchanges about how late or how early we are. The same thing happens to me with my professors, I'm often the first student to arrive, the only one who shows up on time; I greet the professor with a false smile and he takes advantage of the unanticipated intimacy to ask me questions.

Later in the dream we are finishing up a class on some author. The professor has entered into the nervous part of his monologue when he repeats the main ideas in different words, hoping that the charitable voice of some student will offer an opinion or interesting question—he never knows whether he'll have to end class early. In the end, the professor is quiet, frustrated. Just then, someone questions the typology of the novel's spaces. Your ideas are plausible, says the professor, but we can't know whether they're true, because they involve projecting ourselves beyond the text, to speculate about the couple's future, which the author denies us in the moment he writes the word "end." (It seems that I was thinking [in the dream I was thinking, parallel to that discussion], about how the novel was unfair to me, its faithful reader. What happens if I want to follow the day-to-day life of a character who fascinates me, is it possible that I don't have the right to know if, in *Coronation*, Mario and Estela manage to escape poverty, make a family, raise a beautiful daughter? But Estela is finished on the penultimate page, when at last the book reveals her to me as an extraordinary woman, it also takes her away from me, takes her right out of my hands, because I long to carry her with me beyond the confines of the paragraph. She'll never be held by the reader, only by Mario. Alicia, on the other hand: I could get up right now, get on a *micro*, get off in front of her building, buzz the intercom, go up, she opens the door, surprised; she's alone, I pull her to me; pressure, tangible and ephemeral desire, if I so desired. All things considered, I know more about Estela than I do about Alicia. And I'm more adventurous with her, of course, it's easy if the woman is invented, she doesn't have a body. Saying her name in the flesh, Estela, I don't feel the death rattles that Alicia provokes, each breath I use to name her is something lost, a wasted chance to hold her, kiss her all over, to speak and to be silent two inches from her face, breathe her tobacco smell before she departs for somewhere else, some faraway place, for Neutria, for old age, where my hands will only touch her in writing.)

Soon another hand goes up among the listeners in the class. A gringa is talking now. In the face of the general stupor, her question, which is heard out of context, seems to reveal a doubt that was burning inside all of us before we came into the classroom; I smile hearing her poorly pronounced Spanish: "Excuse me, professor, but do you know what happened to the student Violeta Drago?" The professor goes pale, looks at the floor, unbuttons the collar of his shirt. He swallows and answers: "It's good of you to ask. The truth is my conscience won't let me work. I know Violeta's hidden story, she was, of course, a very dear student. It's a tragedy, but I want to assure you that if I didn't say anything it was only because I didn't want to get myself in any trouble. Besides, no one has come to me to talk about it, no one has asked me anything."

(And so, in all my apathetic infatuations, as a reader and as a body, where do I locate the attraction I feel for Violeta? She was a living human being, reliant on blood like myself or any other, and yet she has now become a memory. [And where are the pictures of her, the video footage, the sound of her voice captured on a cassette, her high school yearbook, where is she?] That main character in her deliriums, as fictional as Donoso's monsters, although she insists they were lived experiences. Alicia moves her head, angry. Would I ever be able to get anywhere near that albino girl—though she has appeared so often in my dreams of white walls in recent nights—if she weren't dead? The answer is no. Because when she died, the pages she'd written came to me. [Alicia reads this and says not a word.] We living beings are cursed, we can't know ourselves without the existence of inanimate objects: a novel, a personal diary, a letter. Another paradox: whoever claimed that the dead don't communicate is the one who is dead.)

In my dream the professor kept on explaining himself. "She showed me a few stories she was writing, very interesting. We met at a café on the fisherman's cove. She was ridiculously nervous when she showed up, barely hanging onto a pile of loose papers, she told me they were dreams (dreams within the dream), not stories, and that she couldn't stay to talk because she had to hurry to go help a friend. A friend of hers was going to be killed within a half hour, or have stones thrown at him, or get turned over to the police, I can't remember. She ran off down the street. I followed her of course, in my car at a safe distance. Suddenly I was stopped by the sound of a gunshot. I saw Violeta and a boy clinging to each other, the boy—I don't know if you know him—who walks around out on the quad with his books and notebooks; he was pale from the shot, I already said it, from the bullet that had struck Violeta too. The two kids—I really want you to understand this—were staring out at the sea; like they died trying to catch a glimpse of the horizon of Neutria, still on their feet, bleeding out, rigid, entwined, eyes open to the sea. It was a statue, I don't know if I'm making myself clear: they were the very same statue that's been down on the waterfront for years, do you get it?

Then the class and the professor disappear. I find myself walking along that same tourist stretch, along the waterfront from his story, along the boardwalk of a port city that I wouldn't have known what to call besides: Neutria. I walked for hours. Neutria, now that I write it I understand my vacillation, but I was there; now, when I reread my dream I recognize that salty aroma, that air that's impossible to find in Concón, or Iquique, or San Antonio, just as I imagined those streets when I read Violeta's pages! And in this city there were, in effect, not one, but hundreds of identical statues; in every Neutrian plaza, the same plaster and marble couple, clinging to each other, in all those classical profiles, the demented eyes of Violeta, her hair white against a masculine face.

That Sunday afternoon, in my dream, I sat down on a bench in the plaza, surrounded by adolescents touching each other for the first time, two old people watching everything, a middle aged couple arm-in-arm, a balloon vendor, an organ grinder, children, dogs. From the water rushing out of the fountain that plaza's statue had become, through the bustle of the crowd, a faint voice called my name. I approached the fountain and heard the sound of a small waterfall: it wasn't the bullet, it was the professor; it's not a gunshot, it's a sentence; not a detective novel, but an academic essay, a letter, a prayer. Then another image was superimposed: me and ten people whom I love, around a table. Sitting in the dining room of my old childhood home, in Rancagua. I held a thick pen in my hand, a felt-tipped pen with which I wrote a hundred insults on a plastic whiteboard: "Go away, fucking fuckhead professor, decrepit piece of shit, motherfucking fairy, get out of my body." Someone shakes me awake; Alicia (or J) asks me about Violeta, where is Violeta. I write another sentence on the whiteboard: "Carlos closed the small notebook." Then everyone remains still and reads what I write in silence, and I wake up, furious that I can't remember what it was I wrote that was so important, realizing at last that I am not Carlos, that no one calls me Carlos.

THE NOVEL

That night Carlos slept at his parents' house because he had to watch his little sister. Elisa had asked to use his home studio, she needed to put together some pieces of iron and concrete. Bernarda, a friend from university, who was also taking the opportunity to assemble her project for sculpture class, went with her. By seven they'd finished moving their materials into Carlos's studio. In the living room, Alicia spent the afternoon cutting pieces of glossy paper, which later she'd glue on top of old family photos. Elisa, sitting beside her, stared at the entrance to a house, where two extremely elegant men—impeccable dark suits, handkerchiefs in their breast pockets, starched collars, and gelled hair— smiled at the camera. One of them held a newborn baby in his arms. In the background, the sun setting into the sea, a boat, a streetcar turning the corner, one of the early automobiles. The distant setting sun had already been altered by Alicia's scissors: on top of it she put a flat, orange semicircle. Elisa asked, jokingly, which of the men was Gardel. I bet that's him, indicating the newborn. Alicia let out a little laugh and reassumed her posture of concentration. Gardel was her grandfather, she said; Carlos's grandfather too. Originally these men had been standing in Valparaíso, but now that paper circle was an all-encompassing sun that didn't resemble the sun of that city. It was the sun of Neutria. Elisa sat

watching how her boyfriend's cousin pronounced this unfamiliar word:
Neutria. Neutria still retained a coastal charm, unlike Valparaíso or
Puerto Aysén. Industries had not yet overrun its beaches, a neighboring
city hadn't robbed it of its grasses, its flowers, its tranquility, because
there was nothing, not even a country house, for a hundred kilometers in
any direction. Bernarda asked them what they were talking about: she
brought in some bottles of beer, peanuts, three glasses. Elisa got up and
went to put a tape in the stereo. That night the heat was unbearable.

"Dancing Queen" played at full volume. They'd already been drink-
ing, they were dancing almost without realizing it. Another song and
another bottle of beer, until the tape stopped and, with the silence, came
the certainty that they hadn't gotten any work done. Alicia picked up her
scissors and papers again. Jars of latex paint with brushes inside them
and some plaster figures were waiting for Bernarda, while Elisa, squat-
ting, was coating rusty old pieces of iron with concrete. At a certain point
in the night, a rush of air slammed the door to Carlos's room and, little
by little, the window pushed open. Elisa and Bernarda glanced up and
the tools fell from their hands: a strange face was peering in from the
street, watching them. All three gazes were fixed until Elisa, all at once,
shut the window and the curtains, and Bernarda turned off the light. A
light from the street outlined the silhouette of the watcher on the curtain,
immobile, in profile, waiting for a few seconds. The door to the house
was opened from outside. It was Alicia coming in, she called to them
in a high-pitched voice. She came into the room and sat down on the
floor next to them. She was frightened, she said: before going to bed she'd
gone to take the trash out to the street; she was putting the bags next to
the neighbor's when she noticed a man sitting on the sidewalk, smoking,
staring at the ground. The guy commented that if there was any music
that could wake the dead, it was ABBA. Alicia started walking faster

toward the door, imagining that any hesitation would result in a heavy hand on her arm, then he'd be inside the house, in the darkness. She managed to turn the key, go inside, shut the door, and stay still waiting for the furious rattling of the doorknob. But the man decided to leave. Alicia, Elisa, and Bernarda sighed, they didn't move, they talked until they fell asleep right there, leaning against the wall, huddled together.

THE SENDER

I want you to know that if I die young I'm going to stick around.

Like the foam on a wave photographed in black and white one winter afternoon, a photograph I found in a library book by one of the Corporalists: gray sky, white spots from errors in the developing process, stripes cutting across the photographic paper. And in the background, the horizon, black like a thick wall of water that should still be, should have been, moving, forming part of time, water that will never be in the same position again, a faint glimmer and life, or better, each second's passing reminding me that I'm going to die. The distant glimmer—no suggestion of color, just a glimmer streaking across the black water—is not foam, delicious foam running toward me without ever wetting my feet, foam dissolving in the surf that leaves without leaving. The rocks, another shadow on the sea, I can't walk on that beach; to enter that place is to inevitably leave another place behind; seeing myself sitting on a beach wearing a black dress and dark sunglasses is to no longer see myself standing, naked, walking into the sea, bent over this notebook, dancing with you at a party. I choose one image, I lose the rest.

I recall, or rather I write, a memory, saying that this word, this situation, and this place correspond to the exact moment that I saw you for the first time, coming out through the university's main entrance, closer and closer to death all the time: I saw you coming out in a dozen different ways, if you want to know; you were you and you were other, you were a girl who sat next to me in a class; you took a slight step forward, no, you went down two stairs, you touched your backpack, your hair, you focused on me immediately; there were three or more people between us, you closed your eyes from all the sleepiness, you saw me blearily out here, in the same position I adopt every morning, day after day, my eyes absorbing the slightest variations that have occurred on the university's façade during the past two weeks.

To remember something and to write it down is akin to dying, denying that it could've happened another way. But I'm going to die anyway and I want at least to save one image, I insist, one token that tells me how I lost you, since in your gesture of greeting, a slight smile, it was already stated that in the end you were going to go: the frozen image has to be broken so you can move, so you can come close to where I am. Though the night is immobile—like the black and white photo of the beach landscape I found in the library of my professor, the only Corporalist I ever got to know—you are not afraid to come.

And you wonder why what began as an extensive and well-plotted letter has become a succession of fragments. Without answering, I say to you: when I no longer exist—or no longer exist in these pages but in that which is never lost or burned, that which can't even be called *word* because it lasts, because its meaning never changes, your reading—please, please look at these fragments and understand that what I sought in Neutria wasn't continuity, but convergence. That from the first to last page I wrote, I knew that it wasn't I who initiated contact, nor would it be you who would complete it, just like the postman who gives you this envelope will think he's done his job, ignoring that with the act of delivering my correspondence he has helped bring you closer to Neutria and me closer to Santiago.

I had established a routine through which I was going to render the ekphrasis, an ancient name for the writing of the present: ecstatic descriptions of a situation in which the totality is palpable. My routine, in a few words, consisted of going to write down my observations—in the same place, at the same time (eleven-thirty, ten steps in a straight line past the red kiosk)—of a foreign couple who often sat down to rest, briefly and in silence, before continuing their regular morning walk along the black beach. Of course, many times they—the centerpiece of this, my first picture—did not appear. On those occasions I tried to keep the order intact: I'd begin, moving left to right, in one paragraph, naming every detail my eyes touched, from the sand sticking to my foot to the impassable line of the sea in the background. The idea was to arrive at a description that was undisturbed except at the exact point where the amorous bodies, his and hers, with their tender and gentle—if not weary—movements, interrupted the recursive vision of the ocean waves. Each one of her fingers on his face, traveling slowly down to his neck, completing a movement I might never see again. And three days later, when the couple reappeared, walking, in different clothes and a detail in the expression on their faces acquired from the weight, I mean, the passing of the days, when she asked that they rest for a while and he lay down beside her on the sand, the caress would invariably be distinct, the woman's skin other, the approach of his fingernails different, foreign the wrinkles, the shine, the dryness, the position of a single hair growing at the base of the ring finger that disappeared within two weeks, blending in with the stain on his hand—was he a painter?—maybe a shadow her nose projected onto those knuckles that were touching her, their edges diffuse on that cloudy day.

I was seeking to prove that the shapes their bodies could take in my picture were infinite, unlike the background of the beach which I deliberately tried to describe in the same number of crystallized sentences every time, such that if there were two or three days that the couple didn't appear, the paragraphs in my notebook would necessarily be identical: if the sand on the beach was immutable, the waves changed so much that it was always the same wave. And this way I was able to reduce the observation of the sea to a simple formula; the couple, on the other hand, when they came into my picture, never, not even once, allowed me to repeat the expressions of my description. So, through months of work, I was able to establish in my writing what, in your words, is "my makeshift Manichean vision": across an immortal backdrop, the human couple in constant motion. And I attributed the capacity to fix those two bodies that didn't want to linger in my picture to a noun: benevolence.

In the last days of summer, the beach was no longer the same as in my descriptions. Maybe writing erodes too, in the end it's ink on paper, matter on matter, you know this better than I: a body tends to displace any other body that occupies its space, words end up crushing the silence, and that's why I write you; in the end I'll make that which has no body triumph over that which does, and that is the story, the ostentatious sentences that prevent me from immediately beginning to tell you about my last weeks in Neutria.

I hate your foul-smelling flesh and love remembering when you supported the full weight of your body on top of mine. But no. The night extends outside, in the ugly Santiago streets that resound louder and louder, telling me: you'll never say anything to anyone, your words will be cups, but not cups full of water for the thirsty—your time is running out and the night is long—but cups that slip from your hands and begin their fateful fall; this notebook transcribes the precise instant that the cup is suspended in the air before turning to dust on the ground. It won't be transcendence I attain but silence, because I can't comprehend the way I scratched out, the slaps you put up with in the name of our love—while I wept, begging your forgiveness on a dark and disappeared Neutrian street, bending down to unbutton your pants, but you took a quick step backwards and I, humiliated, mocked your pseudo-Corporalism—the brevity of that memory that in my notebook takes up no more than three words—blow, tears, insult (and before it had been so lovely, when you brought me home in a taxi, we were coming from the university, we'd had our first kiss in the library, a one-second kiss, just lips, I was scared and I felt a wave of blood in my neck, a powerful heartbeat, but a heartbeat)—stays with me so I live it over and over again, breaking up.

Will a wondrous thing that occurred only once—and all too quickly—make sense again when it's repeated ad infinitum? You decide, you've already received these pages, if I am now in eternity or simply in the lines of a novel, as a person, as a persona, as a model; you decide if I die with you in the moment you stop reading me. Who more than you, the Corporalist, would long for our bodies to stay, touching each other, in these pages. Fleetingly me, because I can't write you letters from the beyond or the rottenness, I prefer to call it the triumph of silence—not eternity—so that you forget what I'm saying and stay with my body, so that you put what there is to put where it is missing.

In the last days of summer, the beach was no longer the same as in my descriptions. Maybe writing erodes too—you tell me, you're the one who writes. The couple who had come to occupy the center of my picture stopped appearing, walking right to left across the sand, their movements slowing down before they disappeared altogether, and then my sentences could only repeat the landscape, a wave breaking over a wave breaking over a wave breaking over a wave breaking over a wave breaking. The ekphrasis retreated like the undertow, the picture yielded and there appeared multiple glimmers I'd never seen before, and would never see again: the shape of the wave—breaking in dozens of movements that I could scarcely individuate, much less reduce to the word ocean, because they came and went—disappearing like all the water that falls on you when you go under.

I went home shivering. The experiment had exploded in front of my face, the ekphrasis had revealed itself and I'd been unable to write it. Alicia consoled me when she said my tears confused her, that there was no way to know if my writing had succeeded or failed. Looking me in the eyes, she asked me to let her do a final session, that, in her schoolgirl handwriting, I let her do a final description of the black beach, and then I could keep the results if they seemed useful. I accepted.

The next day, Alicia walked eleven steps in a straight line past the kiosk toward the ocean, she sat down and did her best to find the exact words to describe each wave until they came to form a single wall of water that broke without ever ceasing to break, immobile in the moment that the foreign couple approached, walking along the beach. They looked exhausted; he rolled up his pants and she sat down and looked out at the sea without saying anything. Behind them, Alicia—dressed in a black dress and dark sunglasses as if acting out the joke she'd made: this seems like a job for a private detective—started unsuccessfully to write down every gesture the couple made: she lifts her hand and touches his mouth, brushing away a stain on his face that looked like sand, but then it's darker—her finger's shadow, I suggested, but Alicia raised her voice to tell me no; it's a minute drawing in black pencil—and he's unfazed when she skillfully draws lines on his face, so quickly that he doesn't even discover the pencil against his cheek until she stops, she kisses him and says something in his ear.

You know, Alicia says to me, the two of us trying to fix movement using words and she, the cunt, adds a drawing to our picture, three lines—the sand, the waves, and the horizon—and two points—the sun high on his face and an unknown figure moving off down the beach. That slut ruins our chance to halt what's spinning in circles, vibrating, shaking, ending up on the page convincing us that, nevertheless, the world that falls on top of us can also be suspended. Sky, sand, sea, wave cease falling; they stay still around us and we're able to sit on the sand, dive into the sea, ride the wave, never lose sight of the stars that begin appearing in the sky, and in this way we save Neutria. You know, yells Alicia: that little bitch isn't stupid like us; she draws, tattoos, marks the body she adores with a figure that doesn't change, and no one will ever even turn these pages. Then the couple heard our voices. Their eyes turned curiously toward me, and I could clearly make out their faces; perhaps you can guess whom they resembled. Every morning you went with me to walk on that beach, that day you heard a shout behind us, you saw me walking toward the kiosk and also returning home with the notebook under my arm, looking calm, though in truth we ran at full speed, Alicia and I, laughing. She chided me in a low voice: but that's the boy from the university, the one writing the novel, the one who stares at you in class. You were with him every morning, you little minx. I'm jealous, why didn't you tell me?

THE NOVEL

Elisa came back with two cheap popsicles. Carlos removed the wrapper on his and they ate it together. The other popsicle melted after a few hours on the bench in the plaza where they spent the afternoon. Elisa lay her head down across his knees and without intending to she fell asleep. A while later the cold woke her. It wasn't Carlos's knees that she felt under her head, but a jacket, his jacket, shaped into a pillow. Just before opening her eyes she'd believed she was in bed, but the bench's boards materialized and she remembered where she was. Another false alarm she said to herself, just like when she was little and stayed at her cousins' house in Viña de Mar: she thought she was waking up in her own room in Santiago, but then she heard breathing, the sea in the background, and her Aunt Pepa coming up the stairs to wake them for breakfast. For a second—before discovering that Carlos had left her alone, sleeping in the plaza—she thought that, like before, she'd been mysteriously transported to some hostile place in middle of the night. Nearly desiccated trees, poorly pruned shrubs, the gardener hosing down the street, and the old man pretending to read the paper but actually ogling her, all of it added to her disappointment.

She ran her hand over her face and sat up. A pair of men whistled at her from a distance, at her or at someone else, then disappeared. It was late. Shivering, she put on Carlos's jacket. She stretched her legs out over the gravel and looked around. The old man on the bench had put his newspaper away inside his wool jacket. She looked around for Carlos, she saw some workers playing a game of pickup soccer with a rubber ball. A few of them, freshly showered, had come from the building that was under construction near Carlos's home-studio; some days, looking out the window, she'd see them leave, all spruced up, heading out to a bar. She got up. Her head hurt and she was anxious to tell off that old degenerate: the one who'd been staring at her all this time. She started walking.

Suddenly she was in front of a bar. She stood still, staring at the glass of the display window where the specials were written in white and red marker: half-liter beers 500 pesos, chicken and fries 1,000, beer and a hotdog 890. She looked at her face, still swollen with sleep. For a second, she glanced past her own reflection and a man appeared, drinking a beer, his eyes fixed on the wall. It was him. When Elisa entered the bar, Carlos was watching a pretty girl come in through the doorway and walk toward his table. In the neon light he discovered it was Elisa, her face hard, pulling back a chair and sitting down across from him. She moved aside two bottles that were apparently in her way and asked him dryly what'd made him decide to leave her on that bench, alone and sleeping. Better to have offered her up for a million pesos to the construction workers who whistled at her every time she passed by on her way home. Carlos asked her to forgive him. He gestured to the woman cleaning the mirror behind the bar: one glass, please. All was silent as Carlos emptied the bottle into the glass and offered it to Elisa, who turned it down with a raised hand and a tsk of her tongue. She pushed back her chair intending to leave, but Carlos took her arm and spoke: she had fallen sound asleep when the organ grinder started his song. And he'd experienced an urge to learn the man's name, to exchange a few words with him, after all Carlos could hum from memory the melody the organ grinder played every week in the neighborhood. Then he decided he'd give him a coin—he'd never done so before—with the secret hope that he'd be allowed to turn the crank on the apparatus. It'd only take a couple minutes; he hadn't meant to leave her alone for anything in the world. He'd laid her down on top of his jacket—she was sleeping soundly, he'd said this already—and headed toward the organ grinder, who'd just finished his second melody and, as usual, was pausing for a moment to accept coins from passersby. As he approached he couldn't help but stare at the girl talking to the organ grinder, who listened to her very intently, nodding his head with every word she said. It was the albino girl. The albino girl, he repeated, and he'd seen her face before. Perfectly calm, he handed the organ grinder 100 pesos so he could listen in on their conversation: she said that it was a deal then, that he better not leave her expecting, this comment made both of them laugh quietly. The albino girl said goodbye and began walking rapidly away. When Carlos caught up to her, he asked if she was Violeta, Alicia's friend, and she smiled, glanced up, as if noting his hair color, and nodded her head. Carlos paused. He stared at Elisa, who was drinking her beer now, her eyes never leaving his. She was certain he wouldn't tell her everything. He'd wanted to tell Violeta who he was—her friend's cousin—but she didn't show the slightest interest in his words, I know, I know, she said. They were silent, Violeta turned and walked toward Providencia; she didn't look where she was going, her attention on Carlos, walking beside her. Then he asked her what she was carrying in her hand. A magazine founded by some of her cousin's classmates, she said: they'd published a story she'd written. She handed him the stapled and folded photocopies. A gift. In that instant, as he thanked her and told her he'd read it, Carlos remembered Elisa, alone in the plaza. As if he'd betrayed her, as if he were betraying her, she thought. Violeta smiled for *the first time, she moved her head again and murmured: See you, have a good one. She looked a lot like the albino girl from the novel, the one he'd been unable to find in his notebook; he told Elisa that he'd been thinking about the coincidence of their hair color as he headed back toward the plaza, walking, not running, why lie; she looked just like that unfathomable character that he heard in his head. At the stoplight he started flipping through the photocopied magazine. He was stunned when he read the title of her story: "The Wasted Night" by Violeta Drago. When he told her this, he silently looked for surprise on Elisa's face, and yet he realized how hard it would be for her to comprehend what it was that had kept him from returning to the plaza, what made him go into the bar, buy a beer, and a second, and a third. The title and the plot corresponded to the most well-guarded story he'd ever written, a story he invented the painful night after his cousin's wedding when, in the bathroom, he and Elisa had definitively stopped being best friends. The motivations mattered little, he thought, what was important was that in Violeta's sentences the boy who is in love with his best friend was also named Carlos. Although in her version, the girl's name is Beatrice, like in Dante's paradise and unlike his own medieval tale, in which Carlos is a castle swineherd, Elisa a princess, and the curse is delivered from the mouth of a sinister court magician, who's jealous of the seemingly idealistic yet inappropriate relationship that is beginning to blossom between heiress and servant in the kingdom's springtime countryside.*

In Violeta's story, on the other hand, Carlos and Beatrice have been life-long neighbors in a neighborhood in the fictional city of Neutria. Beatrice is obsessed with the place's legend: in a distant time, where a full moon shone every night, the heir and heiress to the thrones of the two Humalén—an imaginary indigenous people—clans, enemies since the beginning, loved one another in silence; as you might surmise, just like in

Ovid, Shakespeare, and Lovers of Teruel, *their love is as forbidden as it is inevitable. The night before the first rain, when it is customary for both clans to give thanks to the moon for her gifts, the heir and the heiress took refuge in the celebrations, they concealed themselves, they started touching each other; the legend is cut short at this crucial point. And all that's been recovered is a written epilogue: from that time onward the moon made the decision to show her full self only after several nights of darkness, to remind mankind that fullness is fleeting, and perhaps to subject herself to the same transience as everything that shines on the Earth. In the solitude of her house in Neutria, in front of her notebook, Beatrice wonders what it was that might have befallen the heir and the heiress at that celebration that had sparked everything that followed. Whenever they talk about it, Carlos comes up with all kinds of explanations to answer her questions, because—as we already know—Carlos secretly loves Beatrice. Until one night, coincidently moonlit, he gives his neighbor a letter that recounts the denouement he has imagined for the legend: foreseeing that fatality lies in store for the passion of their children, the fathers of the heir and heiress ask for help, each in his own way, from the moon. And she arranges for the couple to be allowed a single night of love: for the din of the celebrations to provide refuge for the lovers this one time. And so it is. But when morning comes, the heir and heiress of the Humalén clans decide to take their own lives in the same tree: never to part again. The moon, furious at this act of rebellion, withdraws her presence from the Humalén. Beatrice reads the page and weeps. She hugs Carlos, they pull apart, look at each other, and touch again. Early the next morning, Beatrice wakes up and rereads the letter. She calls her neighbor to tell him that she never wants to see him again, that they aren't friends anymore. Carlos knew the rest of the story by heart. And he verified this by comparing it with his own version, in which the court magician wants to make the young princess his wife and so he reads the mind of the swineherd with whom she converses in the palace gardens every afternoon: because that filthy mind has no room for friendship, not even a spell would be required to break them apart. In the spring the two of them would meet in secret in some passageway for what would be their long-awaited yet ephemeral—though they might have believed the opposite—night of love. The magician outsmarts himself. While in his version of the story the swineherd is hung from a rafter in the pigsty, and princess Elisa willfully drowns herself in a river, Violeta made the ending more implacable: Beatrice flees from the world, she locks herself in her dark room and is found in a state of decomposition weeks later. Carlos, her neighbor, dedicates himself to his job in an administrative office in the center of Neutria for forty years, no family, no friends, no place to call home. He smiles at his coworkers every morning and never tells anyone the daily agony of the fading memory of the touch, the smell, the body of Beatrice that one night, until he forgets even her name and dies, alone, in a hospital bed. And Carlos said none of this to Elisa that day in the bar. He just ordered another beer and handed her the photocopied magazine. Elisa flipped through the pages without seeing them, until she came to the story and read it. A half-hour later she lifted her head, took a last sip from her glass, held Carlos's hand with affection, and they spoke of other things. She can't understand the coincidences, he thought. She thought: he's leaving me all alone.*

THE RECIPIENT

August 31ˢᵗ

"In an aberrant world where taking a drink, hoisting a chair, or passing through a doorway are acts requiring superhuman will power" (Luis Harss on Onetti). I've decided to stay in my apartment, watch TV, eat, sleep, go out with friends (whomever), have a beer some night with Alicia, or another new friend, a pretty girl I just met with whom I can talk about random stuff, not novels, dreams, or love. Laugh a little. Read the assigned reading for a class, study linguistics, go see movies at an old cinema.

That other stuff is not for me. It's for another.

(I got up late, cottonmouth. My head was buzzing and I remembered that there had been other days that C had shown up at the university with her face ravaged by insomnia; she told me that when she actually managed to fall asleep she dreamed prolonged misadventures and, for some reason, woke up with the need to recollect these dreams, to recount them to her boyfriend, who was sleeping beside her. Of course, when she turned on the light, the episodes vanished from her memory and she was left empty, her boyfriend waking up grudgingly, complaining to her to please let him sleep. So she turned off the light but was unable to close her eyes, she lay there thinking, imagining that she got up, got dressed in the dark, went out, walked down to Plaza Ñuñoa, and went into a bar. There she met an actor from a TV show who invited her to his apartment in a building across from hers. They slept together. At last, in his arms, C was able to fall into a deep sleep, right when the alarm sounded and she had to get up so she wouldn't be late for class.)

If I were to stop writing this diary, I imagine, these problems that are wearing me out would disappear. And yet if I were unable to reread my supposed visit to Neutria, if there were no chance of going back to eat cotton candy in the plaza where the statues in the fountain spoke to me, the possibility of fleeing to a better place than this one without leaving my room would disappear. If I were to resign myself to the smog, to spending hours talking about the flooding in Pudahuel produced by yesterday's rainfall, to spending Saturdays at my grandmother's house listening to my cousins discuss used SUV prices, all excited over the possibility of acquiring cheaper vehicle registration. If I were to write an essay proving Violeta's madness through her texts, her cowardice, or simply a letter recriminating Alicia for the way she attributes her own ramblings to her friend, for using a dead person as a pseudonym. And not see her again. Or dress myself in shame, go to J's apartment, kneel down, beg her forgiveness, tell her I'm ready to begin how I should've; like a man who feels physically attracted to a woman, who grows close to her, gets to know her, they like each other, they go out, become a couple, get married. I'd go work on an estate in Rancagua, she'd be a history or philosophy teacher in some prestigious prep school, we'd have three children and satellite TV to break the monotony, no books. If I never read or wrote again about a lost city—silent but with sea and dogs and children—maybe I'd get used to wearing a tie, getting in my car and communicating via honks of the horn with my fellow office workers, residents of Santa María de Manquehue. Or if I were to get up from this chair right now, get on the metro, get off at the bus terminal and, walking up to the ticket window, boldly ask for a ticket to Neutria, the most expensive you have, if you please. Or if, in the middle of a binge, I were to take Alicia to bed, and her legs wrapped around me were cold, even though her hands are always warm. Or if I were to turn myself in at the Police Investigations building on Calle Condell (where last year I sat with J on the sidewalk to listen to the screams of people being tortured) and declare myself guilty of the murder of Violeta Drago, my only pretext being to find out who really killed her. And if after each of these decisions all I received was a laugh, a mocking laugh.

(Before lunch I called Alicia. We joked around for a while about the detective novel I'd loaned her. Then she asked me what I thought of Violeta's notebooks. I evaded the inevitable by answering that I bet the letter inadvertently delivered to me was more interesting, the one the albino girl signed as sender. Alicia said she didn't know what I was talking about. The letter, I insisted; the letter I'd given her in exchange for her friend's writings. Alicia still didn't understand. Really, are you sure I didn't give it to you? No, what letter? We argued. I don't know what's going on. I hung up, nervous; it seemed like someone was knocking on the door to my apartment. I opened it and there was nobody there. How stupid, why would anybody be knocking when there's a doorbell?

In my mind I reviewed where Violeta's letter might be. In the drawer, no. I went through the papers on my desk, the closet, the disorder on the little table with the telephone. The last thing I retained in my worthless memory was me, sitting and contemplating the envelope, too afraid to open that strange correspondence, even though the mailman slid it under my door. And yet it was a letter from the girl who'd been murdered, my best friend's best friend. Then I thought about what Carlos would do in my situation: open the envelope and read the letter; discover everything that Violeta had written for me, what she'd decided to convey in her own sentences; he'd be unable to take it and he'd run out, I don't know where, that is to say, I do know where: to the home of Violeta Drago, over on Pedro de Valdivia Norte, as indicated on the envelope. Having said nothing to his girlfriend, Carlos was standing in front of the door. He rang the bell. He'd ask the albino girl why she was imploring him to stay with her, here in Santiago.) Action, pure, simple, and ephemeral action. (That of writing: I plagiarize Onetti just like he copied Faulkner, who imitated someone else I don't know.)

◆

September 7ᵗʰ

It's snowing in Santiago. Amazing, I'm lying down and I feel cold. I go to the balcony to check if it's still raining and see the falling snowflakes. Down below a couple is dancing like on Broadway (I imagine); happy, she swings the umbrella from side to side, he's holding her around the waist, and of course they're singing. She opens her mouth and the snowflakes fall (how fascinating to write the word snowflake, snowflake, snowflake, to write snowflake because they are actually falling right here in this exact instant and not somewhere else—where I can't see them unless I force myself, fantasize—in some distant and nonexistent country where it snows every winter, for whose inhabitants the snow is commonplace; this doesn't happen in my fiction when I want it to either. This is tangible, like the difference between writing a love letter and forging Carlos's love letter to his girlfriend, Elisa). The happiness bestowed by the certainty of ice melting in my frozen hand is the same happiness I felt when I looked out and saw that it was snowing. So I ask myself how I might come to touch the woman I love without my hands disappearing on her waist, I ask myself this just because the snow is falling.

Snowflakes in Santiago: an oxymoron. What happens when the impossible occurs in front of my eyes? Other times I would've called it a miracle, and yet it would have provoked the same certainty of being alive that I feel now. One day Alicia asked me, a little drunk and knowing her question to be repetitious and unanswerable: "why is it impossible to write from a place of happiness?" My relationship with her cannot be explained, despite all this verbiage. It's not love (that wasted word), rather a condition that helps me go to bed and to get up, that I insist on re-creating, on masking with other names, on transposing into Carlos's novel, and also on recording in an artificially intimate diary. That which only occurs in our presence, that which would only grow in one way: if our bodies made contact. And that act is outside language's reference, an act (love?) so private and elemental that it breaks apart at the simple attempt to assign it a verb. Not even God (I think now that it's a stretch to believe in Him) has remained in that sacred borderland, which is the unnamable, the unrepeatable. God already has a designation and that's why he fell into these pages, where the word can provide for everything. Alicia and I have no nexus, just the one that appears when I write our names together: Alicia and I. The rest is a painful exercise in nostalgia for what will never happen, fiction is sad because it's not alive, because it requires that I turn some pages for it to exist.

(Why do wondrous things make us feel a need to share them with the people we love? I'm thinking about the time we hiked up a hill in Rancagua, when J and her friend got lost on a different path and ended up stranded on the face of a cliff. Her friend was stuck up there all afternoon, paralyzed with panic; J, on the other hand, decided to climb up to the top and go for help. Knowing nothing of mountaineering, she climbed tooth and nail, at one point believing that she wouldn't make it, that she'd fall into the emptiness and die. In that second she thought about her parents, her siblings, her true friends, about me perhaps, but focused on none of them. On the brink of death, it was the memory of a guy she was hooking up with at the time [I can't remember his name anymore]—and the desire to touch him again, to feel his body on top of hers, to still be alive with him—that impelled her to claw hold of a root, prop her feet against the wall, and climb up the cliff face to safety. At least that's what she told me a few days later, after I'd seen her approaching in the distance, injured, her face terrified; when she spotted me, she hurried over, gave me a quick hug, and asked for help. I understood [although in a fragmentary and divergent way, while I took her by the hand, telling her to calm down, calm down, everything will be okay] the nature of her feelings [what I deduced really was this pretentious]: she felt no affection for anyone, we only mattered on the surface, because in the crucial moment she reverted to the memory of a brief fling, a fleeting [I'm simplifying again, I know] romance [that's how I've always thought of them], instead of conjuring me, her best friend of many years. But later I had the contrary certainty: for J, the individuals who transcend are not those who for years have shared her projects, her moods, ordinary and transcendent events, no, they are those who can give her new experiences of sensuality, who can make her completely forget everything but her own body. This was a disaster for me: faced with eternity or the end, my adored J had clung to an instant of the flesh that would rot in a matter of days. And I [invoking God, the transcendence of her in me, of me in her] voluntarily unravel what I most believed in, the image of her at my side; I wept in the tent, a sleeping bag wrapped around me up to my neck, while the whole campground got drunk, celebrating the successful rescue of the two lost girls. I wept, hating J, I wept because I'd have to get back at her for making me feel this hate.)

Why do wondrous things make us long for the company of others? In photographs and paintings couples stand out against a background of snow, because the relationship between two people begins with a physiological need for warmth, says Violeta in her texts on Corporalism, justifying her promiscuity by inventing a little literary group. Should I tell Alicia about this? No, her notebooks are written with astonishing verisimilitude, different from an intimate diary like this one, where in spite of my pretensions I don't abandon the stereotypes of the novel. Another digression: I was going to comment how, through the window, I watched people come out of their offices and marvel at the snow. How the children were yelling (in Santiago children don't yell and dogs don't bark) so loudly that the houses opened up and families came out to take photos against the immaculate background. The man from the apartment across the street, who spends his days watching television or sleeping or writing in a notebook, got up, leaned out the window, and spent half an hour outside with his arms stretched out, looking at the sky. Like the passersby, who walk, tracking the snowflakes overhead (here no one wants to look at the sky, because it's toxic; the ground is no different, but we inhabitants of Santiago have a particular fixation with concrete). I was the only one who was melancholy, it was sad not to have someone with whom to share the unexpected weather; and then the phone rang. In disbelief, I picked up the device and heard Alicia say: I've never seen it snow before! For a second, talking with her about some random thing, blown away by the snowflakes, I thought I was happy: and the feeling was nothing like what I felt when my body was on top of J's. Under the snow, separated by the telephone line, we could be together, each in our own apartment, watching the snowflakes fall, listening: I was wholesome, diurnal, white like the snow, as if I were pulling my head out of a pit, convinced that kindness is not an empty word.

◆

September 9th

If I'd had the energy to design the perfect story for a novel I would be perfect. I'd be able to become one of those writers who appear on the back cover of an expensive book smoking and wearing a wry expression, if only I were able to weave together a world of a hundred and some odd pages that depended on me alone. But it's too hard. I mentioned this to Alicia tonight and she called me a coward, like I'd done to J on other nights: I can't decline an opportunity to lock myself away in a monastery and go mad while, with adequate care, I produce and polish The Book (rewriting *The Aleph* not exactly in a monastery, but rotting away in a hostel in Pichilemu, not leaving that apartment for a year, spending my empty nights working as a janitor in an apartment complex); I don't know if I should cloister myself in a false priesthood or just forget about reading and writing, find a practical woman, a mechanized job, and live, what here they call life. Attend parties with her, laugh my ass off, drink till I pass out. Planning business deals, no risk no rewards; taking up some sort of hobby of course, let's say, attending movie premieres every Thursday at the theater; going out drinking once a month with friends at a local bar, when I get bored of my old lady. Buy some land near Rancagua. Sounds lovely, doesn't it? No. What I've written embarrasses me, I won't exalt the priests or the engineers, of course, but not the writers, intellectuals, or thinkers of this country either, rather those who are in between. Ugh. In the future, these words will be enough for me, if I persevere. I don't know how to be brief.

If I were to take up a regular plotline and sit down every day and stick to what I'd sketched out, I'd be satisfied, but in the margins of my own writing. I would have sat down in a chair and observed the lives of others and only later, in secret, produced my own silent material. Which (I think) Onetti would defend by saying: "I might be a bad writer, but at least I write my life." To write pure fiction, I wonder how he could aspire to be calm by removing himself from the days of his books, hiding in the pages under the names of different characters. Perhaps he felt the same loneliness as his narrator, the same fictive vice that his own creatures used to invent a lair in order to hide from the painful days of flesh and bone. If this strategy worked for Onetti or Brausen, I can't really know.

Although I admire cowards, I don't want to become the coward that Alicia claims I am. I'm not going to ignore the world because it hurts, to the contrary: the most surprising plot is the one that the days continuously reveal to me. There's no protagonist more paradoxical than Alicia, I'm just dull with the pencil. (And yet, Violeta hid away in her house, with her grandmother, weaving next to the chimney. She sat down at the dining room table with a notebook and described a city more grotesque than this one, nicer and sadder, but full of life; there, without leaving her chair, with pure imagination, she was able to get to know boys whom she'd never meet here, to let them pull her away to corners that were impossible to find in Santiago, because they were occupied by buildings, and cars, and dust.

Or not. Or Violeta came from Neutria every Tuesday on the strange buses she describes, arriving Tuesday around midday, she hasn't left her senile grandmother's side except to visit her only friend in the neighborhood, and to buy medications or bread. Violeta kissed her on the forehead, ate a piece of bread and cheese, and went up to her room. Before letting herself fall into bed, she took a notebook from a drawer to document all of the day's salacious and happy Neutrian moments, not like a fiction, rather like a vital struggle against her own fragile childhood memory, such that by eight at night, in the moment that the telephone wakes her and she goes out onto the balcony to watch a line of cars in the distance, over on Calle Santa María, complaining to herself about the horns and the dry air, she'd be able to open those pages and see that a better place really did exist, a place by the sea, with her best friend and, above all, the boy from school.)

The days surprise me, I should write with the objective that novelty be constant. I was at the university, I went to the library to return a book, dropped it off, turned toward the door, and on my way out, at a distance, caught sight of a very familiar face. In the back of the reading room, J was getting up from a table where she'd set down her books and notebooks. Her bright eyes, her happy smile. We'd sworn not to see each other again, it's better for us, but I stood there, motionless, waiting for her; she came over hesitantly and stood in front of me. Stupidly, all I wanted to do was kiss her and pull her body against mine, right there, that we might travel to a foreign land, the two of us alone, married, old lovers; all I was able to do was open my mouth and say: "Say something, please, say something." And she came close to me, fascinated, like she'd forgotten me and was seeing me for the first time. She hugged me fiercely. She was wearing a winter jacket; I put my face against the fur hood that fell across her shoulders. She murmured something in my ear that I didn't understand, stepped away and, without looking back, returned to her table.

I stood in the hallway staring out a window, my eyes blank, my mouth hardening little by little. I tried to turn around, go up the stairs, and for once tell a woman that I love her, that I do now, but first I had to confront my own ineptitude: she hugged me and I didn't comprehend what she said. Writer—fabricator of inert signs. I can understand Pierce's semiotic treatise, but at the same time I'm unable to communicate with my mouth, to listen with my ears, to taste with my tongue, to receive an embrace. Words alone, words don't give warmth. I don't want to be a solitary writer in this room, nor, like Violeta, to scribble (feverishly) that any heat in Alicia's lips, in J's lips, against my own, cannot be written; only that she sees me writing this and wants to read it.

THE NOVEL

Carlos and Elisa and kept in touch with just a couple phone calls: she answered and couldn't conceal the fact that hearing his voice made her happy, saying his name, Carlos, with actual surprise, but then immediately seemed to recall a promise and went quiet. Then came the silence. Carlos couldn't take it and asked how she'd been, what she was up to before he called. Elisa responded, fine, nothing special. Then he told her his cousin was going to Europe, her parents had given her a ticket to make up for who knows how many of her birthdays when they'd been faraway and had forgotten to even call her, poor little Alicia. And as he was saying little Alicia, both of them were recalling all the times that Carlos held her around the waist and called her his little Elisa. She asked him to stop: I already know about Alicia's vacation. He felt the desire to surprise her, by reading what he'd written that afternoon for instance, a story without beginning or end about an old woman and old man who, every afternoon, after lunch, have the habit of going and sitting on a bench in the plaza; any plaza, Plaza de Armas, Plaza de Avenida Perú in Viña del Mar, Plaza de Sucre and Miguel Claro, it doesn't matter. They like to sit there, hands laced together, and watch: a young couple meet, the next day they kiss, and many nights later the girl appears alone, weeping because every bush gives off the odor of that rotten relationship. And beyond, a group of kids on bicycles chase after a dog, a married couple looks around for the child that doesn't want to arrive, the man selling cotton candy doesn't return, but is replaced by a man selling helium balloons, and then by a third man with Styrofoam airplanes. The girl who was crying in front of the bushes is now carrying on an animated conversation with the man who one of the boys on bicycles had become; they get married and grow tired of their oldest son, who escapes from them because there's no other way he'll be able to meet up with the group of adolescents who are making fun of the old guy selling Styrofoam airplanes. The younger daughter, widow of the bike shop owner, buys for her grandsons—no longer children—two bags of popcorn that someone is selling from a truck decorated with neon lights. The old woman and old man do not age so long as they stay in the plaza, so long as their hands remain locked together at the hour of the siesta. This is what Carlos had wanted to read to Elisa, but not over the phone, because as soon as she guessed that it was a story without an end, she'd interrupt and tell him she was sleepy. She'd say it, stretching out the vowels, like she was about to fall asleep in the middle of the conversation. And then Carlos would regret having opened the notebook, believing that he could guess what her response would be if he told her he was going to read something: she'd murmur, as if she were waking up, that if she heard another word about the albino girl she was going to hang up the phone. The silence seemed to last a long time. Elisa asked him if he'd called to have her read his mind; actually, to listen to you breathing, said Carlos. She hung up.

THE SENDER

Alicia changed the names when narrating certain events, when fitting them together for me, one with the other, inventing stories that made her laugh while I sat and watched the boats that went out fishing at night in the port, incessant little lights. She liked coming up with sarcastic lullabies inspired by whatever I was doing, this little light is going out, going out, going out, for The Little One who doesn't sleep, doesn't sleep, that's what she sang; I listened to her from where I was leaning on the railing, contemplating the illuminated port of Neutria, working, waiting for the ring of the telephone to rupture the nocturnal silence and for it to be you on the other end of the line.

She said she preferred to adopt the indefinite voice of fairytales in her stories in order to, just for the fun of it, alter the names of those who appeared to me each day. And yet the next morning she said that she didn't want to use real names of people, because it made her feel repulsive, repulsive words used again and again across the centuries, sullied and cleansed by each and every life, like the windows of a house clouded over by the contaminated air of its inhabitants, like the crystal glasses of a busy locale that—from years of washing—are bound to break, like my hours, like this pen, like my voice.

Alicia was talking behind me and laughed loudly again, she was fixing her hair, about to go out and swim in the ocean, to watch from afar the boy who left the university at sunset. I ignored her; I didn't want to get worn out, I enjoyed sitting still, watching the way Neutria moved. Alicia gave him a name—He Who Is Writing the Novel—when she peered in the window of his room, which faced the street, and saw him remove a notebook from a drawer, tear out some pages, and sit down to write. I didn't want to know that she'd seen him buy a new notebook, transcribe a few of the torn-out pages, date several sections, and, with distinct hand-writing, begin to write the following: Starting today the novel will dictate my days; my days will be embodied in these pages, these pages will be embodied in me, and I'll be embodied in an other, until this other can no longer be embodied and the novel ends. Even though I didn't want to hear about it, that night Alicia came out to the balcony anyway, to tell me stories about how he watched me and wanted me, wanted me the way an author wants his protagonist, with a longing that demands an end, and this isn't just a manner of speaking, silly Violeta, I've seen how he spends sleepless nights writing the story of an albino girl to whom some-thing fatal happens. Then I laughed at myself.

We'd seen each other almost one year before, we were classmates in a literature course at the university. But I'm sure that we've met each other long before, somewhere else: a plaza in different city; you're a little boy, you approach the edge of a fountain because a supernatural glimmer at the bottom catches your eye; you are deeply disappointed because through the water you see that it's the light of the sun reflecting off a coin. I'm a little girl, I approach you with great curiosity because you've stayed in the same place for so long, but I can't see what you're seeing, I'm much smaller than you. You turn around, you find me on tiptoes and ask me what I'm looking for; the bottom, I say. At the bottom of the water there's just more water, you say.

Then you go. And I believe you.

The professor of the class where we met liked to repeat that literature is a laboratory, and on one occasion someone asked him if by this he was referring to the naturalism of Zola, he concealed a mocking expression and said that we should follow the etymology: literature as a space to labor. I was left with a feeling of something missing, of malignance, by the discussion of the nature of the written—like everything that seems to have no end—and when everyone was leaving, I approached the professor to discuss this. But before I could say anything, I found the eyes of He Who Is Writing the Novel, standing beside the professor; a heavy sensuality came over me, I'm not sure if it was prompted by the professor or the student. According to Alicia, as I walked away, the professor said something in a low voice and He Who Is Writing the Novel raised a hand in my direction, leaning slightly, then lifted his other hand and pointed at me, and then, quickly, let both arms fall, unsettled by the professor's words: That is a body. Alicia maintained that neither of them smiled, but stayed serious; the boy stared at the floor and lifted his arm for a third time to sketch the movement of my feet walking away in the air. The professor, on the other hand, looked directly into the eyes of He Who Is Writing the Novel.

The next week I lost all interest in the lights out in the port. Alicia sang: the little light has gone out, where is The Little One, find me The Little One. I lost interest in my classes at the university, too, and concentrated on the composition of my second picture. Just like how every now and then I hear footsteps approaching the door to this house and get up to look out the window, pretending to be focused on the trees moving in the wind, but actually sad not to have welcomed you with this finished letter, until I sit down again to write you, it happened then, when the voices interrupted me at the exit to the university and made me turn around to see who was saying my name. Then, just then, I was at the right distance from the façade to realize that I had discovered my second picture, the one that would at last sustain the ekphrasis: in a landscape that is purely human—I said to myself at the exit to the university—nothing will stop; but a construction that people enter and exit will be different. I believed that once I wrote about the persistence of a single building and its inhabitants, the eternity of all of Neutria would not be unthinkable.

What I'd never considered is the illusion upon which the ekphrasis is based, which came to me suddenly when at last I gave up writing the paragraphs that I was using daily to describe the façade of the Universidad de Neutria, repeating the same succession of images, the same nouns, the same verb. Actually, it was Alicia who revealed the illusion to me and planted the doubt that would again give rise to the movement of the characters, that would alter them by putting these words in their mouths as their only reflection: this action might be my last. When she came up to me complaining that she was bored of my stationary routine, asking me to at least let her read my paragraphs, she almost touched my face with hers trying to understand the smile provoked by my final lines: He Who Is Writing the Novel takes a step forward before starting down the stairs that give way to the path of smooth stones leading to the university gate; around him, the pointed arch frames the blackness of the tall entrance to campus; the stones are interlocked in a formation that is rectilinear in every way up to the metal lettering that displays the name and the year the university was founded, flanked by two gargoyles, leading to a barely discernable curve that bears toward the depths of one corridor, the wall at the back from where it descends to a basement whose classrooms hold up the edifice of thick beams and old concrete, covered by the plastic tiles that support the right foot of He Who Is Writing the Novel, who balances on the edge of the first step—while one of his hands tightens the shoulder strap of his backpack, his hair falling straight across a forehead that hasn't a single wrinkle, the origin of the skin, the smoothness of his forehead extends across his face, twisting along the tops of his temples, reaching his neck and covering his clavicles, his arm, part of his fingers, his fingernail, not a hitch in the movement of the hand that opens, not a crease on the shirt, not a mark on the face clean as the marble that half covers the walls at the entrance—and moves toward someone on the steps who has made a false move, who is losing their balance and falling, no; he walks toward the gate with a stack of papers under his arm, copies of a magazine called *Suspensión*, one of its sheets still folded across his butter-colored shirt, which, in spite of the wind and the quality of the fabric, isn't wrinkled or stained; one of his eyes slightly closed because the sun is hitting his face, the half-closed pupil stares straight ahead; I'd say that the angle of his right foot with respect to his leg is too open, exaggerated, he doesn't seem to be walking; I'd say that his only wrinkle is the eyelid above the contracted pupil, I'd say that He Who Is Writing the Novel sees nothing as it falls.

After reading the ekphrasis, Alicia bent closer to my ear: liar, the only artifice is in the eye of the girl who watches, in her cold eye, for she doesn't want to know that blood still circulates through her, that above his head the shadow of a leaf is falling, detached from aromas of the university entrance; that if the girl is a light, all lights go out; that the ekphrasis is writing and all writing is linear, it has to end, it ends like the silence, and like the circulation of the blood that pauses to keep my eye from lingering on the image of He Who Is Writing the Novel, not because his young body is now floating in a glorious state of permanence, but because he slips on the step, clumsy, disbelieving, and goes down, his head cracking open against the only solid thing, and the running blood hurrying to finally stop running.

He stumbles. Catching himself when his pupils manage to look up and see me once again: she's been sitting there writing at the same time every day since we returned to classes. He Who Is Writing the Novel decides that his experiment is ending, he won't come through that gate again to see if the albino girl is watching

him, because—when I stand up in the moment he loses balance—
he has proven that she is. He comes over to tell me that he's writing a novel in which the important thing is the persistence of
bodies, in which, he'll tell me a few weeks later, he asks himself
what would be left of me in him if he'd managed to touched me.
I'm afraid, alone, and attracted by that hand as it rises toward my
body. Alicia's intervention shatters the picture, and those pieces
begin to move with me until they attain the velocity of my writing, so fast that if you or I fall to the ground we won't ever be able
to say that we got up.

He Who Is Writing the Novel waited for me to dry my mouth
enough to speak before smiling, warming up, putting his arms
around me without making it overly obvious that he wanted to
touch me, and he said: what you're doing is precisely what I'm
unable to write. According to him, he needed me to speak concise-
ly about a painting that interested him greatly, in a text that would
be read in public, because it would form part of the manifesto of an
artistic movement that would leave everyone in Neutria, everyone
in the world, with closed eyes—I expected him to say with open
mouths. He said he needed my help, he looked me in the eyes and
then, don't ask me why, I kissed him quickly on mouth, just lips.
He Who Is Writing the Novel was stunned, repeating barely com-
prehensible phrases; that love and work don't mix, like soul and
body, I responded, trying to help him, but he was speechless. I
promised I wouldn't touch him again, that we wouldn't spend our
time fornicating whenever we saw each other. He trembled and
in that moment I really loved him; I loved him like a child, that's

what I told Alicia. Like an adolescent would be better, she specified. Perhaps that's why her stories are incomplete.

I haven't told you about my earlier visits to the professor's house yet. He had invited me over twice before you took me: Alicia came along both times, she can attest to the fact that the professor did nothing to force me, rather it was I who told him to stop talking as I got on top of him, not caring anymore about Alicia's eyes on the painting of a beach and its waves that occupied the entire surface of the living room wall; the armchair was moving, the sea was no longer restrained by the strokes of the paintbrush—I knew then that it was the professor who'd painted it—and it began to recede and get me wet. I admit that the professor's mouth irritated my lips, yet his hands grew old and then vanished when I turned my back on the ekphrasis: yes, at the cost of my degradation, of the physical effort to separate body from soul—*delusion* from *delight*, we called them as little girls, laughing, me and Alicia—the painting hanging on the wall breaking apart in time, along the opposite path I was going to perpetuate the intangible. And then, before the wave painted on the wall broke with its powerful aroma, I got up off the professor's body, got dressed, washed my hands, looked into his old face to verify that he'd planned the whole thing: I was just a useful body, he said to me the first and the second time. In particular I remember his fingers pressing against the wall where he'd painted the seascape, the soft way his index finger slid across the line of the horizon when he asked that we forget about what'd happened, and this explains why I felt nothing the afternoon He Who Is Writing the Novel invited me to visit the professor's house so we could look at the painting that he wanted to write about. Just then I realized that the wall where the oil of the seascape had mingled with my sweat a few months before had been meticulously blotted out, and over it there now hung a small canvas.

I don't expect this letter to become a series of notes about my life, I'm not going to tell you about how I get up, come and go, climb the stairs, and enter the bathroom with nothing to do there, stare at myself in the mirror so I don't have to look at my actual self. Violeta is my enemy and Violeta is me: alone in my grandmother's house, abandoned by Alicia, waiting for you, but you won't be coming to hold me, to cover me with your body and its heat. Though it's guaranteed that you will come: you'll open the door, and without approaching you'll touch me from afar, I'll fall down wounded, me alone. And at no point will you have moved from the doorway. I just need for you to imagine that I raise one hand from the notebook, that you take it, that together our fingers collapse on the bed and stay there, entwined; if I become something more than the dead body at the beginning of your detective novel, the pages will open up so that any person walking by on the street can look in and stand there motionless watching how I'm writing at this table in the moment that you open the door and take aim.

THE NOVEL

Josefita had pulled back the covers of her parents' bed and lay down to sleep and watch TV until they got home from a dinner party at the house of some friends. Mesmerized, she checked the time on the bedside table clock when she was woken by the sounds of the car parking, the key turning in the lock, and her father's voice saying something. She buried her face in the big pillow to seem soundly asleep while hearing every single one of their interminable footsteps, until her father lifted her in his arms and she understood nothing yet knew perfectly well that they were carrying her to bed.

Carlos, lying next to his sister, pressed a button on the remote control, searching for a movie on TV. Josefina had gotten up and was pushing open the closet's enormous sliding door; she knew her mother kept her grandmother's trunk, a couple of fur coats she never used, and a whole collection of family photo albums in the back of the closet. Carlos asked her what she was looking for while she silently flipped through the albums one by one, tossing them onto the bed. Written on the covers, in their mother's lovely handwriting, was the year the photographs were taken. Ugh, said the girl, too old. Carlos said nothing, thinking that in those garish snapshots he was more or less the same age as his sister. Josefa continued doing her thing: she'd open an album, catch sight of the first photo and toss it aside impatiently, picking up another. Apparently she wasn't looking at the photos for the fun of it, even though she loved doing that too; instead, Carlos deduced, she was trying to find one photo in particular. He repeated the question: what're you looking for? Josefina paused and said, one from when she was a baby. He put a photo in front of her from when she was around a year old, with a spot of hair and a surprised expression—taking your first steps in the living room of the house in Pocuro, he explained. She immediately opened another album, closed it, grabbed a third, protesting that she was already big in that one, that she needed one from when she was a newborn. They reviewed the photos carefully and could only find Josefina smiling at the camera, two years old, with a beach hat and chair on the sand; a dozen similar polaroids: her yawning around five, raising a hand around three, waking up, eyes barely open around four years old. The girl twisted her mouth and sat down silently on the edge of the bed, staring at the TV. Carlos waited for her to say something; he knew she wasn't paying attention to the movie that'd begun about an hour before, she was thinking about something else. Without turning around, she muttered that she knew she was adopted. It took Carlos a second to understand what she was saying and then he smiled: Don't be silly. Josefina turned to face him, furious, like he was to blame; then why wasn't there a photo of her as a newborn like everyone else has at home, she said. Carlos responded calmly that she shouldn't be so stubborn, that he'd seen her in the clinic, bald and red, less than a day old, sleeping in a cradle next to their mother, who, because of her, was very tired. That she shouldn't be ridiculous, she looked so much like their father and like him. Josefina got the point. She'd never really believed she was adopted, what happened is that her friend Cata's parents, just last week, had told her that they weren't really her parents, and all because she found a photo where she appeared in the arms of other people.

Carlos got up to go to the bathroom. While brushing his teeth he yelled to Josefina to put the albums back in order. Elisa had told him once that, when she was little, she'd thought she was adopted too, all because her older siblings liked to bug her with jokes about her dark hair and nearly nonexistent nose. Since she wasn't blonde, she wasn't part of the family, they'd repeat. And she invented an alternate identity so as not to feel hurt: her name was Carolina, a name that in her childhood she found particularly melodious for some now faded reason, a name given by her true parents, benevolent people who lived in another place, in the country of the good people. One day she was playing with her ten siblings in the garden of a house that looked a lot like the gingerbread house she'd seen in an illustration of Hansel and Gretel, when the imaginary country was invaded by the neighboring bloodthirsty nation. Her parents were killed in the upheaval and, in an act of desperation, the firstborn brother loaded her and all her siblings onto a boat, and they were able to make their escape. Indescribable adventures led them to many of the world's ports, where different families would grow fond of one of the siblings and beg the firstborn to let them adopt the child: who wouldn't want to raise one of the last remaining children from the country of the benevolent people? The firstborn believed he'd be able to ensure the happiness of all his siblings, giving them away one by one to interested parents, and yet he wasn't always successful; often the natural children of these adoptive families were envious of their kindly nature and teased them, like what happened to her in Viña del Mar when she was taken in by new parents, given a new name. With time, Elisa had come to understand that she was just as boring as her siblings and didn't really belong to some benevolent race. And yet, as long she was unable to come up with a just fate for the oldest brother, she would never forget this children's story: she imagined him in the most absolute solitude, old and dejected on a dilapidated boat, looking out at the immensity of the ocean before the breaking of the storm.

THE RECIPIENT

September 13th

Still too tired to really get into it. And yet it's important that I continue to record the unbelievable storyline of these days; without ceasing to read, without ever closing a book, I decide to go out into the street to recover whatever is still alive of Violeta Drago in this city. It's stopped raining at last, the dark clouds have receded, and the days are getting lighter. Without purporting to get up from this chair or put away this notebook, I spend the days walking toward Pedro Valdivia Norte, the neighborhood where Violeta's house is located. Friday I was leaning on the railing of my apartment balcony, not moving; the whole afternoon I was in that same position, staring dangerously at the ground, many floors below. None of the solutions seemed right to me: not the morbidity of Arguedas and Lihn writing their death diaries, not Onetti and Violeta inventing a city where they run away from their own ruin, and in whose streets their characters find no relief from suffering, but do find oblivion. Keeping in mind that the impudence in these pages was my solitude's only saving grace, aware too that I write these lines to be read, hoping only that someone will be able to understand what I cannot. With the suicidal compulsion to put this notebook in an envelope and send it to J's address. But I already said that she's going to disappear, like me in front of a desk, surrounded by towers of books and worn-out pens, piling up. Only Alicia, because the name I've given her here isn't her name and doesn't do her justice, will survive. (I realize that she doesn't fit here, that she can only look in and never enter entirely, or follow along for a few pages, because this notebook is in error, hardly one true word.) Just Alicia versus The Little One. Alicia during the day and The Little One late at night: me, drunk, I can't help it that first one and then the other appear on my right, on my left; my uneven Manichean vision. And like Carlos, I try to bring them together in an embrace, as if I were the center of everything: me and my pen describing this three-way relationship such that The Little One, lying down, was reading a story in which the protagonist pays for her parents' nursing-care by working as a whore, exclusively group encounters. That's what The Little One said to me, the one who was reading an anthology of stories and poems for a writing workshop at a university in some southern city. In Neutria.

When I rang the doorbell at the house on Calle Los Araucanos, it was she, The Little One, who appeared. She asked me what I wanted: she was holding a book in her hands, dressed in pajamas, her short hair in disarray. I lied, telling her I was Violeta's friend. She returned my look, disbelieving, had I come from the south perhaps, she said. The south? Why the south? Your naivety is infinite, she repeated all night long, when she wasn't biting me. In that moment I said yes, somewhat inhibited by the brightness of the house, by the decorations Violeta and The Little One's grandmother had used, by the silverware, by the ceramic animals, the fake ivory, the yellow lamps, and the acrylic plants. The Little One put the teapot in the kitchen and led me to her room. Her grandmother wasn't home. Had she been waiting for me? Had she been waiting for someone else? The unease on her face when she took off my clothes, she'd probably felt obligated to open the gate when I told her I was Violeta's friend. Then I asked her if they really were cousins. (Why does she live in Violeta's house and stay in her room, so talkative, such short bones and rapid movements, the opposite of the figure that weeks of reading Violeta's infernal handwriting had created for me?) Yes, of course, The Little One said: Yeah right. And she went into the bathroom. I stayed erect. I was entering another body, another city, at last I was emerging from the pit, I say, of this apartment.

Hours later she came out of the bathroom, drying her hands, and asked me my name. Carlos, I continued to lie, as if that very afternoon I hadn't been pulled from paralysis by Alicia's phone call: she told me it was important that we see each other, not about Violeta or my novel, but about her and about me. (About us, responding without being cheeky.) As if I hadn't spent that very day thinking about putting a bullet in J for what she'd said to me when I called her, ready to start over. As if I hadn't spent an eternity leaning on the railing, watching the raindrops fall more heavily than yesterday and the day before, playing with the idea of locking myself in my room, not sleeping not eating not watching TV, not waiting for the days to fabricate this book for me, but forcing myself, like a maniac, to write a facsimile-novel of *A Brief Life*, substituting my own presence for Brausen, J for Gertrudis, Santiago for Buenos Aires, and Neutria for Santa María, but never finding in that facsimile-novel a character corresponding to Alicia, to her role of impartiality. Then she called me. I put on gloves and a scarf, expecting that it'd be another afternoon of indecisive conversation; Alicia would try to keep me from getting obsessed with her (or with her friend of the notebooks), I'd want to believe that her teasing was intended to get me to make the first move, to stand up and kiss her and pull her far away from this dusty city with my madness: I exited the elevator promising myself I'd destroy all of it after a few beers. Of course she'd react to my violence, which would at least give rise to a story of another sort. But no, it was preferable for me to remain still, hearing her neutrally over the telephone. I thought that Carlos, that he would act in the exact opposite way that I do. That I should have never given Violeta's letter to Alicia, since it was addressed me. I closed the umbrella, raised my hand. The *micro* that was coming, splashing pedestrians, wasn't the Providencia *micro*, it was the one that went down Kennedy directly to Pedro de Valdivia Norte. The moment I got on it I became someone else: with the certainty of having stood Alicia up, I stopped in front of the door to the house on Los Araucanos and asked for Violeta. I regret nothing, I regret nothing.

◆

*September 20*th

No one regrets nothing. The last memory I have of J (if that was the last time, because her writings are very oblique) is of her raising one hand in shy greeting, from a distance. I couldn't imagine her, despite the determination of her words: shrunken but in no way fragile, her long fingers energetic in the air. The other seemed to be oscillating between his notebook, his book, his pillow, the TV, the telephone, the balcony, and all of a sudden The Little One was clawing his skin and he was unable to hide because he was naked in the middle of an unknown city, maybe a consequence of nothing more than the inexperience of our poor narrator. (I know that he'll come and rewrite this, one, three times, but at least I'll dedicate myself to writing about my own life.) Or maybe he's lying there in bed, half asleep and trying to focus on a photocopied article of criticism on Onetti that he's reading, thinking he's abandoned the writing of his so-called personal diary; while reading about the notion of uprooting in *A Brief Life*, his desolate eyes fall on the drawer containing this notebook, wrapped in brown paper, and he thinks: another precious project that never materialized. The idea had been to defy Alicia, that a novel fabricated with the uncomfortable and carnal plot of the quotidian would be more excessive than all the scribblings of a little albino girl, who abuses her body to gain access to that imaginary childhood city; he couldn't have known that the passing of the hours would turn against the writer, chaining him to everyday life. O, how I adore those types of figures: the one who writes in isolation triumphing over the one who lives constantly thinking about what is happening. Unfortunately I am subject. I live here, with someone who has fallen asleep, who is starting to dream about snow, about the idea of purity. The Little One enjoys this, looking up at me panting on top of her, saying: "Carlitos, you still believe in purity?" And I stroke her face with both hands, with the backs of my fingers. If I speak the learning will cease; I should moan, breathe, cough, clear my throat and spit on that little girl, whom I despise and adore simultaneously, stretched out naked across the wrinkled bedspread of the moth-eaten mattress where she lies waiting for me. She gives me a sign, putting a vertical finger over her lips and together we draw back, watching him; the expression his face is wearing now is very entertaining, leaning on the desk, ripping out a page from the notebook where he has written the following:

◆

September 20th

I spent the 18th at Alicia's house; her parents weren't there. She invited me to dinner with one of her cousins and his fiancée. The conversation was very interesting, she was gorgeous coming back from the kitchen with a tray full of sushi and everything arranged so she'd always be sitting in the empty seat next to me. She avoided looking me in the eyes, turning her back on me whenever she could. She had an artichoke leaf in her small teeth and she wanted to hold my hand, rocking one leg, the same combat boots as always, sometimes brushing against one of my shoes, the left, and announcing in a serious tone that this was a celebration, the reason didn't matter, better that way, right? For a second, let's pretend that we can be other people, that a space exists where we could be happy, the pain of the pen leaving its mark. Let's leave behind for a second this thing about you and me, about literature and possibility. I was going to say that it'd be better for us to forget that she was Alicia and that I was me, sitting there with such affection, such longing, such love (that word), that we lost the names, that I am a false resident of Santiago, that she travels every month and every week, but where is she going? That when I attempted to write an *authentic* page, her albino friend got raped in the paradisiacal port of Neutria by a group of beggars who found her under a bridge without any clothes, all because of her longing for transcendence, a twisted need to escape the skin. Alicia was widening her eyes, listening to me, then she interrupted, exclaiming that she was nervous because her brother had taken her parents' car out right in the middle of the September 18th festivities, and some drunk might've run into him. I went home, I was that drunk, and I brought her smell with me, asking myself how I could possibly keep from getting obsessed with a woman like her, thinking about her black dress, about good and evil, about the body and the soul (the blathering of drunks). How not to want her, how to understand why she evaded my touch, I don't know, for the same reason that J asked that we just be friends, because the flesh ruins itself, the touch becomes abrasive, the orgasm ends, not so a conversation between a man and a woman who guess each other's words, complete each other's sentences, invent expressions, laugh at their own verbal ridiculousness. Thinking this, I got in bed, tried to masturbate, but felt like a child, went over to my desk chair wanting to touch something in this apartment that wasn't mine, I opened my eyes knowing what Carlos would be doing now: sleeping with The Little One, or, at least, dreaming my wet dream about her.

The Little One listened with a silent, little laugh to the way I imitated that guy's monologue. Then she unclasped her legs, which were wrapped around me, got dressed and said: come on, Carlitos, it's Fiestas Patrias. We're going to find the others, we're going back to Neutria, without Violeta, who cares about her. Let that other guy sit around and worry about the dead albino girl, not understanding that she was trying to leave but was just afraid to do it on her own, and that no one knows how to interpret those pages she wrote about the Corporalists. Don't look at me like that, you don't understand anything either, who's going to shoot her if she's already dead, stupid. She was so beautiful.

Then it was dark. It was a cold night, we were walking toward Cerro San Cristóbal, and into my mind came his rueful face looking at his notebook, uselessly recovering the thread of his diary. A static image like the last one I have of J, and so it's not a surprise that he stays like that, like in one of Alicia's drawings where, sitting in the quad at the university, she and he observe J approaching in the distance, and in turn J is watching them: all three with their hands in the air, waving. The characters understand that they'll never touch again, that they'll only be able to wave to each other from far away, and The Little One and I pass through a gate that opens onto the part of Cerro San Cristóbal covered with bushes, at last we make out a naked hand holding a cigarette that rises to guide us.

THE NOVEL

Carlos remembered a summer when he was about fourteen, a girl in Rapel. He would dive into the lake and then run back to his towel. The girl, he didn't remember her name, spent entire days lying there, wearing ridiculous dark toy sunglasses, reading a book; there were times when she didn't appear for days and other times she'd spend a whole week just a few feet away. When he came back from swimming, numb, he felt like he was being watched. Once, Carlos asked her what she was looking at, the girl said nothing. The next day he tried a different tack: why was she looking at him. She responded that it was because she desired to look at him. Just like that, over and over, without variations in the dialogue until, at the end of the summer, Carlos had approached the girl to invite her to go waterskiing at the reservoir on his friend's boat. She thanked him, but said she had no desire to go. Desire! Carlos exclaimed mockingly, and went running toward the pier.

He saw her again a year later. Rapel was emptying out, it was the last night of vacation and Carlos was sitting alone under the spotlight on the wooden pier with a can of worms and a fishing line. Every now and then, in the dark of night, he made out couples walking together, groups of children, fathers unable to sleep because the next day they had to go back to Santiago, back to work. After a while a girl, one or two years older than he, sat down next to him, looked out at the still water and slapped one foot, chasing away a mosquito. Carlos looked at her out of the corner of his eye and, despite the fact that she wasn't wearing those hilarious sunglasses, he recognized her as the girl from the previous summer. She asked if any fish were biting. He shook his head and considered saying that the only thing biting him were mosquitoes, but didn't. The girl threw a rock into the water and then apologized, maybe throwing stuff in scared away the fish. No big deal, said Carlos; she stood up and took off her clothes so fast that he barely saw her as she jumped into the water, swimming out into the lake and coming back immediately because it was too dark, she said. Carlos offered the girl his hand and she climbed up onto the pier and sat down beside him again. He said that it was really cold to go swimming; she'd felt the desire, that was all, she said, gathering her clothes, shivering as she disappeared toward the houses. He hadn't seen her again but, lying there on his bed, he remembered her features perfectly. He had a desire to kiss that distant mouth, to bite it. Then he went and looked out the window: there was no one in the street.

THE SENDER

It's hard to put in order what was said at the professor's house, when He Who Is Writing the Novel led me by the hand to look at that painting. It's hard because I've never transcribed a dialogue, because dialogues don't exist, no, what exists is a multiplicity of voices that don't always correspond to the people opening their mouths; sometimes they aren't even speaking, and yet we hear them. The professor was waiting for us on a soft armchair, legs crossed, a whiskey on the table, the aforementioned painting on the wall behind him. The professor greeted He Who Is Writing the Novel with a wave and looked me right in the eyes, waiting for me to look away, ashamed, but I wasn't at all perturbed to find myself so composed in the same place where previously I'd been writhing and sweating. He Who Is Writing the Novel removed a great quantity of pages, notecards, and biographical clippings from a folder that contained the professor's research regarding an unknown Neutrian poet from the '60s. The money He Who Is Writing the Novel's family sent from Santiago to pay for his studies came late or not at all, and the professor offered sizable sums to students who compiled information about writers of particular academic interest, demanding their complete discretion and erasing any possibility of ever sharing credit for his publications with them. Truth be told, He Who Is Writing the Novel never took himself all that seriously: the professor published his student's annotations verbatim. A debt of some kind existed between the two of them, and because of this the professor had allowed me back into his house.

At first they were discussing their latest discoveries, but couldn't come to an agreement. For my part, I considered the pain I could cause the professor, while fixing three more whiskeys and drinking them, chewing the ice and scratching the surface of the sofa, ignoring their conversation. They'd spread out dozens of pages across the surface of the coffee table that summarized the different versions of the biography of Our Young Poet, which is how they referred to the subject of their research. The professor was nodding, parroting certain paragraphs out loud, asking repeatedly about some irrelevant detail; so there was nothing left for me to do but get more ice or flee to the bathroom, where I voiced questions that Alicia would then respond to in the mirror: how to make the professor but not He Who Is Writing the Novel disappear, I said to myself, after splashing my face with water. Returning to the living room, I found them taking notes for the official biography of "Our Young Poet," and I sat down to read their pages. I remember little besides a few sordid milestones from the last months of his adolescent life. Enough of this nonsense, I said, it wasn't funny to play at writing new chapters of *Heinrich von Ofterdingen* if Novalis himself had wanted to leave his novel incomplete, but He Who Is Writing the Novel stopped me, gently removed the glass from my hand, and, coming close, kissed me, the bastard. Truth be told, Our Young Poet believed Novalis, he believed Artaud, he believed Lautréamont, and he proclaimed this in meetings at Casa del Escritor, in lectures at the Municipal Library, in confessions to friends who were casually studying journalism: you should only write in extreme states like rage, drunkenness, anxiety, pain, and sickness, he said. Although he'd published two very short books when he was sixteen and seventeen years old, he was praised by poetry experts who never wrote a single verse, and when someone insulted him, calling him "regurgitated Rimbaud" at the reception for an award, he felt so understood that no one ever saw him again; sticking to the Rimbaudian plan like clockwork, except that on his desk he left behind too many clues. If the boy had left behind a posthumous work, then all this mimicry was just a farce or the concealment of something more, I said to them. He Who Is Writing the Novel responded that in light of those final pages, Our Young Poet had decided to give up at the last minute, impelled by a horrifying discovery. Then the professor gave me— with his bloodstained hand, bloodstained sooner or later—a photo of The Young Poet at eighteen, pictured with his father and an uncle at sunset in Neutria, between neighboring houses, a street that dropped down toward the port and, in the background, the sea, the sea, the sea, the sea, until He Who Is Writing the Novel took the glass from my hand, helped me up from my seat, we took two steps and stood facing the painting that hung from the white wall: a multiplicity of faces appeared between the brushstrokes, faces that swarmed under a ruined bridge, barely illuminated by an old lamppost in the foggy night, next to the black river; the fleshless faces of the beggars appeared, their heads bald and pallid, each one the same as the next. The enigma was that only one of those imprecise faces belonged to Our Young Poet and they were all identical to the photo the professor showed me.

Just like at Alicia's party, where we saw each other much later on, I raised my glass—full, immediately empty—to protect myself from the light and to see, through the glass, your face glowing in two distinct ways. Then I had to touch you, to be sure that the radiance emanated from your skin and not from the surface of my eyes. At the professor's house, unlike at the party, I set the glass down on the table with great care and began reading the poem that you'd handed me by Our Young Poet: stanzas that told, almost without verbs, the story of a beggar who knocks on the door of a mansion where a Decadent party is being thrown; the host, an enormous fat man, was describing the dinner's obscure dishes to his guests: octopus with purple cabbage and beans, oxtail soup, eggplant in toasted sesame sauce, roasted legs of lamb with caviar and dried mushrooms, beet flan, blackberries, seaweed, and chocolate. For a few seconds, in the enormous fat man's ostentations, I could see the tricks of the professor, smoking on his sofa, belt unbuckled, legs crossed, eyes half-closed, one inert hand, pointed in my direction. He Who Is Writing the Novel ran his fingertips down my neck, the enormous fat man was getting dressed to specially welcome the intruder who, according to the acrostic formed by those verses—"AWAITING ANOTHER GUEST"—was coming to infiltrate his party, while the whiskey, like the anxiety, was making me sweat, seeing the movements of the host as he stretched a silk sock up over his adipose left leg, bent in front of a burnished old bed, where five naked adolescents were drawing near to lick his spine, mine; the votive candles on the tables had consumed themselves down to their pearl holders when the lovers' muscles contracted in front of the ash and the wax that a very tall woman, veiled in lace, standing at the foot of the bed, let fall from the cigarette and the white candle that she held in her hands. Then the enormous fat man adjusted his perfumed, blond wig while wrapping each of his fingers, voluptuously, around the knob of the front door. The heavy wood opened slowly and, suddenly, with the cold of the late night, a set of claws clutched the edge of the door, which the enormous fat man attempted to close with mock terror. In that moment, He Who Is Writing the Novel was talking about the poem's lack of synesthesia, about how it was impossible to feel the stench, the filth. And the professor corrected him, without taking his eyes off me: the purulence, the pages and pages describing those filthy men whom the poem calls beggars; their flirtations with the exclusive guests on mattresses in dozens of bedrooms, the bleeding who cried out for mercy in the hallway, with open arms, smiling. The final stanzas, more concise and lyrical, stayed with just one of the beggars: one who advanced through the flames that at dawn were consuming the mansion, until he came to the door of a room that was still intact: when he entered he could scarcely see anything, every vase, every table, every chair shone brighter than gold. Almost falling down, blind, he was able to comprehend that it was an optical illusion caused by hundreds of mirrors and one candelabrum. He blew out the candles with a single breath and, although the fire had reached that room too, he paused, enraptured in front of a canvas that hung on one wall: it was the portrait of a large group of filthy men under a bridge. The poem ended with a dialogue between the beggar and the tall woman with the veiled body in the middle of the fire. The beggar managed to take down the canvas and roll it up while telling her that this was the final work of a painter who'd gone mad, who'd disappeared from the art salons after putting the finishing brushstroke on the canvas that the beggar now held under his arm, revealing to the woman that he was himself this very painter and that he'd come back to reclaim his work: he'd had a vision of his future once, he'd decided to paint it though he remembered little, and yet he couldn't bear what he saw emerge from his own two hands. The woman let the lace fall from her body and approached: but now you're with me, inside a mansion in flames; this wasn't the image of the future that appeared to you. The beggar covered his eyes with one hand, clutched his painting with the other, and ran. Until he tripped.

I looked up from the book, I saw that the hands of He Who Is Writing the Novel were far away from me, clutching the chair. But how can you not understand that this is what's most important? He shouted, furious, the guy decided to put his resolution in writing! The professor offered him money to keep something a secret and He Who Is Writing the Novel fumed that a time was coming when those who write would be able to defend that something. I don't remember exactly what they were talking about, because I found myself somewhere else, on my balcony, looking out toward the port of Neutria, seeing myself in the light of a boat, in the night; I was leaving and Alicia was waving goodbye to me from a distance, her hand high in the air, leaning on the railing of the beachside boardwalk. I know that later He Who Is Writing the Novel was singing the praise of Corporalism and its founder, Our Young Poet, while I climbed up on the sofa to remove the painting from the wall and take it. The professor was so scandalized that he demanded we leave his house immediately.

Days later, He Who Is Writing the Novel buzzed the intercom at my apartment and asked for me. I heard Alicia's laugh, she didn't want to tell me who it was until he was already standing in my door, moving his hands up and down, nervous. I didn't want him to come in my room, so I led him out to the balcony so Alicia could observe us calmly from the living room, while we turned our backs to her.

He Who Is Writing the Novel looked haggard. He took out a notebook and pen, sat down in one of the chairs, and told me he was about to fall down from sleepiness, because he could only write at night and in the morning he had to work and to study in the afternoon. He chose one of the chairs facing the sea. I already wrote this: I'm exhausted too, the words are leaving me behind, I can't stop myself and the place where I come from, the place of the first lines of my letter––the simple story of my love for you in Neutria––is behind me; so I turn around––because it isn't just movement that exists here, but the obligation to write "so I turn around"––and I delay in picking up the pen and again the words are behind me, like trying to touch something at the center of my own spine, unattainable yet mine alone. Alicia lost patience when I began to digress: better to get yourself two mirrors, put one behind you and one in front, open your eyes, my God. I got angry too: so why was she there, then. More than once, I'd held a hand mirror in front of me, turning my back on the big mirror in my grandmother's bathroom, without success: behind me I always saw Alicia, never the nape of my own neck.

125

THE NOVEL

Carlos found a torn-out page from his novel on his desk. He was surprised to see it there, discarded, and when he read it he was baffled: it was a page from an old notepad, which he'd glued to the back cover of his notebook, where in two paragraphs the detective story made its first appearance and which one day he'd crumpled up and pitilessly tossed in the waste basket; the character left his house on a Sunday morning to buy the newspaper, still unsettled by the sleepless night he'd spent unable to produce a decent article for a crime-story magazine that had offered him a job. Not only would it be enjoyable to read the travel supplement and the reports about economic conspiracies, he could also find material in the police report, which offered detailed analyses of all kinds of crimes on that particular day. He crossed the street and paid the old man at the kiosk, turned around, and traveled half a block flipping through the headlines. On the corner he saw the figure of an albino girl, tall and thin, wearing a summer dress and carrying a notebook in one hand. He considered the paleness of her skin.

The red light gave way to green and the girl crossed the street; just then a car accelerated, not paying attention. She froze, the car didn't even brake when she let out an ear-splitting scream, brushing against her and disappearing two blocks down. The albino girl fell to her knees, covering her face with her notebook. He asked her if she was okay, helping her up. When he stepped back a little, he saw that her tear-stained face was scrutinizing him. She murmured something incoherent, maybe a whimper, and then, as if he'd been the one trying to hurt her, took off running. He was left standing in the middle of the street, not knowing what to think. He found the albino girl's notebook on the ground and picked it up. He walked home thinking about coincidence: just before the accident he'd actually wondered what it was that girl might be writing in those pages.

Carlos stopped reading. He recalled that earlier in the week he'd heard different people say that coincidences don't exist. But what would happen if a third person forced someone to realize those unknown desires, he wondered, even if it was an accident. In that first version of the novel's opening, the character had wanted to help the albino girl and yet he'd ended up delving into her pages; he thought about Elisa, about himself, and about the albino girl Violeta. He also reviewed the pages he was writing now: convinced that the killer would act that afternoon, the protagonist ended up shooting the girl, passing from investigator to investigated, from innocent to criminal with a single nervous movement of his hand. Someone's eyes pulled him from his reflections. A man was watching him from the street, standing in front of his window; he didn't bother to draw the curtain, instead he noted in the margin of the torn out page that the man's face and eyes resembled his own. And when he looked up there was nobody there. Leaning on the window frame, he scanned the sidewalk for the man in vain: it must've been a neurotic, some passerby who wanted to examine the expression on the face that watched him obsessively from the window of some random house. When he was five years old, Carlos *was convinced that every night a stranger watched him from the hallway while he slept; the paradox was that, if he stayed awake to prove there wasn't anyone there, the terror kept him from lifting his head off the pillow and looking out into the hallway. Until he fell asleep.*

THE RECIPIENT

September 21ˢᵗ
4:15 A.M.

"Biblical statues tasting the salt in our own mouths, twisted and borne away by the wind in the movement of turning around, and yet, for a second joyful statues, nonetheless." (A phrase shouted over and over in my dream, my own cries wake me and oblige me to write this down.)

◆

September 24ᵗʰ

(Every muscle in my body is tired. This is a final attempt to stay on this page. I could force myself to sleep, I could stare at the ceiling all afternoon, I could just let the phone ring [like right now], wondering who's calling. I hope it's Alicia, but know it's not. She reappears a few days later when I've already slept off the intoxication of her and not even a trace of her mouth remains, talking to me between ironic laughs. I bet it's some company calling to sell me something, or my mom reaching out to say hello, or some friend wanting to grab a beer. I want no more nights, no more sleepless nights, just radiant spring days lying in a plaza, the smell of freshly cut grass, Alicia's quick, possessive eyes looking at me; her short eyelashes that make her seem like she never sleeps.)

The Little One asks me if I want to see her friends again. Of course she was emphatic; she was confirming that I was as fearful as she thought after the way I reacted on Saturday, when I left, running down the bar's stairs, disgusted and bewildered, but not afraid: fear, that sensation that precedes sickness, disaster, disintegration, is a resource for those who need preparation for things. I've always been direct, right when I'm about to explode I open my eyes as if I'd slept from sunrise to sunset, and my own inability to prepare myself for the worst always surprises me. On Saturday, heading down the path that leads to the abandoned part of the hill, I found shreds of clothing, crumpled up papers, candles, kilos of hair, unused videotapes; The Little One had told me before about the Corporalists, that the boy had been expelled from the Universidad de Neutria after putting on that spectacle in the middle of the quad, the day that Violeta wanted to come ("to die" they told me) to Santiago. The story of a depraved professor, of a fake erotic manifesto written to take revenge against someone, I'm not going to spend my time talking about what happened or about their reason for fleeing to the one city they most hated, because there are things she won't tell me yet. The curiosity led me to take the hand of The Little One, and I believed us to be in the middle of a field when suddenly we appeared on Américo Vespucio and the cars did what they could to avoid hitting the running drunks. I'm keeping the rest to myself, I'll just add that when I woke up

I was so sick I could barely lift my head; I bolted out the door of that dive bar, I couldn't look at the stairs anymore, exhausted and puking, I went out into the street. Sunday morning, downtown, I don't remember the street name (Puente, Catedral, Ahumada), all I heard were a few bored police officers harassing a beggar, sleeping on a bench; the cries reached my ears and I couldn't comprehend why they were hitting him, nor could I distinguish between the cobblestones that passed before my eyes as I started to run. I couldn't help recalling The Little One's contortions on top of the table in the bar, the fat body of the man who cornered her against one wall; I understood that my decision in the spring to be someone else had come to an end at the point in the night when the Corporalists started to play word games and make bets; when the boy said *delight*, The Little One took off her last article of clothing. I woke up that Sunday afternoon in my own bed and allowed sleep to pull me away on other adventures where I wouldn't stop to consider the implausibility of a phantasmagoric Victorian intrigue unfolding in my uncle's country house, where an albino girl, fierce (sum of sums), and I were the only suspects in our own murder. I saw myself getting up the next day, slow and thirsty, I saw myself sitting in front of the notebook, the fucking notebook made everything stand still, the notebook where I watched myself lament not finding the precise expression to narrate the character's disintegration.

(Last night's party was in an old bar downtown, where an acquaintance of Alicia's was exhibiting photos of monsters drawn by a childish hand, tempera and pastel pencils across the walls of squalid public bathrooms. A rapper improvised exclamations in counterpoint to two cellos and a violin, while backstage someone simulated powerful electronic rhythms with their lips and throat so that at the climax a tenor sax drifted out from behind the curtains. I'd escaped this apartment at last; in my inertia I'd thought that—since I needed to buy a new pen so I could keep on writing— a walk would be my only respite: I wanted to write until someone found me collapsed on top of the page, to wake up in a white bed, to have Alicia come visit me in the hospital and, before leaving, for her to confess to me that she'd been the one who'd found me at the desk, my face streaked with ink, that she'd called my parents, and that before the ambulance arrived she'd gathered together my pages and gone home to read them in peace. She wouldn't hate me for speaking of her to the infinite (blonde, brunette, short or tall: the same idealization), she'd understand and yet she'd feel a little fear. Fear. So much fear, in fact, that she'd let my period of convalescence elapse without visiting me, forgetting about me, writing a little novel copied from my deliriums. (Forgive me, she'd write on the envelope that'd come to me in the mail.) This is what I wanted: for the world to destroy itself if I enumerated every part of it. For Santiago, so destitute in the empty pages of my diary, to at last be filled with inhabitants, with a river and a history; I thought that I should get up and go out to buy a pen, but the intercom buzzed and I jumped, frightened. It was Alicia, she was downstairs in the lobby, and as usual she wanted me to go with her to a party. I had to come, she said. I closed the notebook, got dressed quickly, walked to the door wondering how much of me would still react to the bodies of other people.)

We laughed. What, she thought I was going to stay inside sleeping because of the disgusting behavior of some drunks? Or better: The Little One and I laughed as we ran down the stairs and got in her car. I grabbed her around the waist to kiss her, she twisted away, without taking her eyes from the stoplight at Américo Vespucio she asked me not to be a coward today, at her friend's birthday party. Be quiet, I responded; it was just that, a couple nights before, I'd been dumbfounded to see her like that, on top of a table surrounded by executives toasting a fat man, who was vomiting bile, glasses breaking on the floor while her hands were pinned down onto the sharp edge of the table by the knees of a man wearing a tie. The man had approached her, run his fingers along her fleshy arm, and whispered something in her ear. He'd call her later to have us join them in a private room. What name had he uttered in that moment? She didn't answer. We parked, went up to the house's gate, knocked. No one came out to let us in for quite a while. The Little One looked at me, I took her hand and squeezed it, demanding that she tell me her name.

(I danced with S almost all night, we had a good time together, thrilled by the stupid movements extremities make when there's something driving them: music that takes hold of the hips and arms and chest, as if a different type of pounding blood animated us and the autonomy of the organism were lost when confronted with this pulse that comes from outside, that connects and disconnects us not only to the person smiling in front of us, but also to the couple whose backs touch ours because of a misstep, to the passionate kiss over there in the corner, to hands that form bodies when brought together, and to the mouths that open yet say nothing; there's only one body that's separate, Alicia's body, dancing around whomever she likes, never in front of them; she joins a circle of bodies clapping their hands for a wild dancer, comes toward us, makes a half turn and I don't want to smile; I smile at S, the three of us dance together, she's lost again in the confusion of heads and necks. When S goes to the bathroom, I stay on the dance floor and Alicia reappears beside me, distant because we're never able to bring our movements together to form a single figure, a figure that moves forward, draws away and comes together and laughs, but never stops. The body is movement, its only rest is death or dreaming: Alicia and I discussed this the other day. Now, on the other hand, when we try to dance, the silence is the moment I trip and almost fall; in the blank spaces of our conversations each of us reproduces the true message on our own; I don't understand what it is she's doing, but I marvel at the confusion her movements provoke in me. I go up to her and kiss her: there's no possible interpretation, I'm separated from you if you stop reading these words and start dancing; Alicia moves away, she's disappointed by our stiffness. Later I find her sitting down and offer her my beer. Why the long face? I ask. She answers with a monosyllable and I, without having planned it, respond with a phrase that she likes. The moment is overwhelming: she and I in the absolute ubiquity of our dialogue, I think about how much I love her and for an unexpected second she rests her head on my shoulder. All of a sudden we realize what we're doing, we shake ourselves and talk again about some random thing; the contact provokes separation.)

The Little One didn't want to tell me her name right away. She opened her mouth with surprise, but then a blond man appeared and invited us to follow him through the gate without saying a word. Later, she licked my ear a little as she told me I could call her whatever I wanted, and I was delighted by that party where dozens of couples groped each other on the couches. With my hand on her back I led her to the center of the living room. She came close, put her arms around my neck, and we swayed to a soft music. It must sound different from how it was; the Corporalists of Santiago rarely use words. They were there to enjoy themselves, The Little One explained. Mouths opening only to share their partner's mouth, tongues fulfilling their roles while fingers weren't instruments, but parts of foreign bodies, like the knees, the waist, the neck, the eyelids, the groin. A solitary woman fell down, asleep; she was useless there. A man lifted her in his arms, she curled against that unfamiliar chest moving off to one of the bedrooms; the two of them were sleeping deeply in one of the beds; or maybe he was shaking her violently, then came a slap, she shoved him and ran crying out to the patio. At the end of the night, the couple lay peacefully on a rug in a room on the second floor: it's love, The Little One interrupted at sunrise, when I told her that I'd spent the entire night thinking of the perfect names with which she and I would be happy.

THE NOVEL

It was very early in the morning. 5:15, Carlos saw on his watch. He turned the key, pushed open the door, groped the wall in search of the light switch and turned it on. He contemplated the living room, briefly illuminated, then flicked the switch again to proceed in darkness. He bumped into a potted plant. Tired, sad, and drunk, he let himself collapse onto the couch and closed his eyes. He could still hear the shouting inside the car of the friend who'd offered to give him a ride home. At Salvador and Providencia they'd spotted two transvestites. His friend had slowed down to get a look at the fairies, he found these girls fascinating from a distance, he said. He said to look closely, they were paragons of woman: legs long as columns, those waists, oh, those waists. Of course their hair was a little strange, but those shoulders, those shoulders in the air. The car crept up the incline; the two transvestites approached one step, then another. The problem, according to his friend, was that everything changed at a few meters; it was a problem of distance. Now those exquisite women had turned into garish men, costumed and painted, serious faces giving way to nervous chuckles and then fits of laughter, he added, accelerating. In the rearview mirror, the shrinking image of one of the transvestites panting, furious, open mouth insulting them: sissy faggots. From desire to laughter and then the leering faces, the weariness, the silence. The problem of distance, of the lie the head tells the eyes, and the eyes tell the touch. Like what'd happened to his girlfriend, said Carlos, interrupting the silence in which they were moving. Like the problem Elisa had when that gringa with whom she'd exchanged letters since she was thirteen came to meet her in person; she hadn't had the courage to tell her unknown yet intimate friend that she disliked her shrill voice, or the strange acidity of her scent, or her emphatic hand gestures, that she came too close when starting a conversation or blinked slowly whenever responding to a question, moving her head up and down. The truth is that Elisa only relaxed after dropping her off at the airport, and that the feeling had been mutual: she never received another letter from the gringa.

Carlos didn't know how long he'd been sleeping on the sofa. Outside the first songs of the thrushes and the roar of micros starting their routes could be heard. He unbuckled his belt, unbuttoned his pants, kicked off his shoes. It was cold. People's bodies didn't disappear when they closed their eyes, he thought. One time he had convinced that same friend to go drink with him in his car, parked near the exit to the club where Elisa and her friends from school would often end up when they went out. They talked, watching conversations between the bouncers at the door and guys who were trying to get in without paying, a drunken brawl that ended with ambulances, the shouts of an intoxicated kid who didn't want to surrender his car keys. Suddenly another car that was parking caught Carlos's attention, especially when a group of girls climbed out. Her: the one with short hair, a skirt, quick movements, and an invisible nose, he pointed. He was about to get out of the car to greet her, ask her name, and give her his phone number, who knows. You're an idiot, his friend said: how had he not realized that it was Elisa, arriving with her friends.

THE SENDER

That morning He Who Is Writing the Novel showed up at my apartment, yawning, with circles under his eyes. He had to see me, to talk to me; for the first time he said: I want to tell you about Corporalism. I kept hearing I want you, I want you to know, that his words wanted to use mine, that he was going to say things for me, the silence that goes unwritten when there are two authors. And there are always two. In that silence Corporalism was already formulated, before they were introduced to it in the auditorium at the Universidad de Neutria, even before you sat down in your room to write the novel that would serve as a guide to the Movement of the Body and the text enslaved you.

Alicia and I had convinced ourselves that sooner or later He Who Is Writing the Novel would come to our apartment on the pretext of picking up the story that I'd promised him at one point for the third issue of his photocopied magazine. I lied to him; never in my life had I been able to write something with a beginning, middle, and end, I'd never put a single letter of mine on any page that wasn't the transcription of a dream or an attempted ekphrasis, so I went to Alicia and asked for one of her short stories. We made a deal: one of us would sit down and write and the other would publically present herself as the author of eventual features in magazines and books, to receive the praise, give thanks, and put on a good face for the critics. It was fair. My pages are not easy to publish; Alicia's stories, on the other hand, might interest certain readers obsessed with children's literature. So I selected a pathetic fable entitled *The Wasted Night* and gave it to He Who Is Writing the Novel. Later he blushed when, on his way to the elevator, he turned back to look through the open apartment door and noticed that I was waving to him from out on the balcony with one hand in the air, while behind me Alicia was gesticulating with all her fingers: at first glance it looked like obscenities, but then I realized she was sketching a small glass sphere inside an elastic and translucent globe that was closing in on its center. Soon the globe would explode and, with it, the sphere, before we could make out the face reflected in the glass. I closed the door to the apartment and Alicia shook me harshly, her hands on my shoulders, so that I understood: the man hadn't come for our story, she said, he's going to lose those pages because he wants a different narrative, one in which you and I are just the names of women he likes. Mark my words.

Days later, He Who Is Writing the Novel buzzed the apartment intercom and asked for me. Alicia answered and he said: I'm coming up. Because he needed to see me again. He knocked on the door, I came out of my room fixing my hair, half asleep. Taking the wrist of his right arm I lead him out onto the balcony, and we sat down.

He Who Is Writing the Novel looked out at the sea. His head and his hands moved back and forth, he couldn't look away from the rolling of the waves; I, on the other hand, sat in front of him, my eyes fixed on his face. Sometimes he crossed his legs and I'd grab his hands to keep them from moving; other times I'd look back into the apartment, where Alicia sat in an armchair, her legs crossed too, holding a cigarette in one hand and a book in the other. Her fingers kept separating, slowly, then the coming back together, never quite making contact. Then my gaze moved from her to my own barely perceptible reflection in the glass, then to the face of He Who Is Writing the Novel. Objects were injuring him, he said. Suffering from insomnia, he decided to get up and try to leave his room, he ran into a wall and ended up on the floor, his head cracked open; he started writing frenetically and one of his fingers slipped on the surface of the pen and he cut himself on the edge of the page. He was bleeding.

I stopped writing for fifteen minutes. I went out to the patio to see how the night was spreading over the garden, its stars concealed by clouds and a dry, scarcely perceptible, summer wind. Since then, not even closing the big windows and the curtains has been enough to keep me from feeling that wind; I felt heavy, I could barely keep myself from falling asleep on top of these pages, sleep again. Sleep as an alternative to permanence and death, the dilemma that has led me to write this lengthy letter. Sleep is an alternative, He Who Is Writing the Novel said to me, haggard; he slept in fits and starts because every three hours he had to return to the notebook on his desk; to leave behind all forms of writing is death, my Violeta Who Is Writing the Novel, he was saying, stretched out across one of the chairs on the balcony. Because there's no other way to stay here besides slicing yourself up into various characters, who nonetheless—because they all belong to a single body, to me, the one who is writing this right now—struggle to be reunited. The characters move away from each other and disappear from sight, getting lost in the narration and, contemplating the landscape of the story that awaits them, they decide to return with eyes closed, running, only to collide with the others who are approaching them at full speed. Those who survive the impact remember nothing, they don't realize that they've grown or that they were bigger before, and they begin to wander through these pages without knowing that they're preparing for the next collision. Finally, after many pages, there's only one left: one who has endured all the blows, who traverses valleys, oceans, deserts, and mountains without finding anyone, until he sees me, the one who is writing. Every night through the window I see the character coming toward me. He approaches at a run. He reminds me of so many people I've known, more than anything he resembles me: he's a woman. And yet he's not a woman, but someone who is not a man, someone who will appear at the end of my novel and demand his death or my own.

Then I asked him a question that neither of us could hear because I couldn't get it out of my mouth. I was lying on top of He Who Is Writing the Novel—his words emerging disconnected as if in a dream, the murmur of the sea mingling with his voice as he stroked my head with one hand—when he started to tell me what the novel was about.

For two entire nights of insufficient sleep, he wrote the novel, until he closed the notebook with a start, terrified by the possibility that I'd actually died in the final fragment. He left his house and came running to see if I was still alive, frightened that he was fulfilling his puerile desire to have the written turn material. The novel was something else, new and the same as always; the novel in which he opens the door, I look up from the pages of Neutria, and then I'm dead on the floor of my own house, was a novel-manifesto, he said: the novel of Corporalism.

He was the protagonist. He used his own name or simply He Who Is Writing the Novel, depending on his mood. He reiterated his own physical features, those hands that were too much for him and that I sometimes held between my own; again and again you enumerated the stages of the novel-writing process, and during the book you split into two, three, even four. You asked me if I'd fallen asleep, I swallowed a sound that signified yes and adjusted my position against your chest. You kept one hand on my head and another on my back, you were smiling because my slack body was at your disposal, what you didn't realize was that your hands were also prisoners of my weight.

He Who Is Writing the Novel had resolved to carefully follow the movements, alive and dead, of The Young Poet: that his body had been found in a grave of disappeared people, that he might have ended up a beggar under the bridge, just as he'd predicted in his own posthumous poems. Waking up I asked him if he really believed that the painting we'd found in the professor's house had been painted by The Young Poet, by his adolescent hands that experimented with rhymes. He Who Is Writing the Novel tried to get up to find something that would verify his suspicions—an article by an art critic, a photo, a reproduction of the painting—in vain, all my weight was still on top of him. I'm an obstacle, he said. I asked him again if he really believed this;

he kissed me and answered: my little skeptic. I couldn't laugh in that moment because he had one of his fingers between my teeth and I didn't want to make him bleed. He added that to follow closely the path of one writer we couldn't pretend to be inside the skin of another; and since he hadn't had the privilege of being The Young Poet, it occurred to him to write down a plan so that anyone else would be able to trace his steps. A map, he summarized. He would describe the passage from writing to simulation—and from simulation to application to belief—that The Young Poet had followed. I looked out at the Neutrian sea, at the old houses near city hall, the buildings, the forest, the old port and the new one, the park, everything visible from that balcony, and thought about what he was saying: to tell how a boy writes verses about a character who paints the portrait of a beggar to in the end become that beggar, that character who paints, that boy who versifies, that narrator who narrates. Or instead to memorize the verses, hold the paintbrush, say that among the portraits of beggars that one portrait exists, give everything away, stop eating, remain silent when spoken to, go to the bridge, convert. Divide an author into his characters just to see if it's true that in so doing you can arrive somewhere far away. And once you're far away, recover the author in the characters from a distance, insignificant; be The Young Poet. To achieve this he had to imagine how he spoke, the way he moved, to what extent he faltered when he walked. That was why he needed to write a novel, to follow one writer until he became another writer, never the same one. It's just that there would come a point when it would become impossible to deny that something false was sustaining the project, something that would make him lose all motivation, put his notebooks aside, do nothing for hours, months, years, until his own indolence ended up turning him—definitively, without words—into a beggar. And I, sleeping on his chest, confused what he was telling me with a dream in which the inhabitants of Neutria came, one by one, to enter me like a rented costume left on the floor after a party, while Alicia continued to smile at me from the living room of our apartment. I woke up when He Who Is Writing the Novel removed his hand from my hair, upset because I hadn't paid attention to him, asking me why I arranged things to always hear the same words, as if I couldn't understand. As if I were stupid. And it was always the same for me: character and author, the sea and the shore; our boat and the dock from where we just set sail.

Alicia got up from her armchair, hurt by the way He Who Is Writing the Novel was treating me. The afternoon sun reflecting off the big window blinded me, and yet I was able to see her take a chair, climb up to the top shelf in our closet, and pull out a large suitcase. I was alarmed.

I heard the voice of He Who Is Writing the Novel mixed with other voices, adult voices, serious, busy, absent: voices that spoke of literature, of how admirable it was that young students continued to participate in cultural activity. A deep voice indicated that the important thing wasn't to write or to read, but to publish; it didn't matter what you made so long as you made something. A sharp voice made reference to money available for State creation grants, the need to fill this city lacking in history with stories; someone similar to He Who Is Writing the Novel agreed, and someone else, also similar to him, listened very intently to the advice they gave regarding the earnings a young writer could expect if he gave up writing in favor of plot, like on TV but in a book. Two writers who'd been published and honored in other countries entered through the door to the university auditorium, found their seats and sat there drinking without saying a word to each other, despite the fact that they'd known each other for more than a decade. On the opposite side of the auditorium, the students were finding glasses of wine, touching, and occasionally, between fits of laughter, flipping through previous issues of the student literary magazine that was being presented that afternoon. A man, identical to the one talking on my apartment terrace, had to cover his face and sneak off to the bathroom—his expression was a grotesque laugh, a wail—when the rector commented that he probably wouldn't have time to read that issue of the magazine either, but that he was still grateful that they'd sent the previous editions to his office, and that he had no doubt about the quality of the students' contribution to the cultural profundity of the institution. The lights were slowly coming down.

The professor watched me from a distance through the glass of red wine he was holding against his forehead, without waving, without flirting, without even asking. I observed all of the boys identical to He Who Is Writing the Novel behind the long table, manipulating microphones, slurping their shimmering cups of water without really drinking, making their teeth clink against the glass. Beside each of them was an albino girl, a face overly familiar to me; and yet I was sitting at the back of the auditorium, and, through various altercations, I'd been able to keep the seat beside me unoccupied for Alicia, although I imagined that she wouldn't be showing up again in that auditorium or anywhere else at the Universidad de Neutria. With arms crossed, He Who Is

Writing the Novel read from the pages he'd left strewn across the table in mock disorder; at his side was another boy, just like him, who rested his head on his hand and smiled, ironically, thinking about the unanticipated public turnout at that presentation; and there he was again in front of the microphone, eyes directed to an empty spot in the corner of the room, and again head resting on the windowpane, sitting on the floor, everywhere. He was searching for my white hair in the audience and yet in his hands he held the hair of an albino girl who was sitting beside him; I adjusted the microphone on the table at the event, trembling because my finger wasn't finding the switch or because the audience would hear my ragged breathing, my gasps, my ignorance: what was I doing there if I couldn't remember Corporalism, if I wasn't able to get ahead of the facts of the novel being told to me by He Who Is Writing It. The lights were coming down in the auditorium, little light, I saw myself small two places farther back, in front of myself, there to the left, to my right, behind; I was grateful you hadn't wanted to come, because you never stop talking and that would've made me nervous.

He Who Is Writing the Novel squeezed my hand, looked at me from the podium, cleared his throat, ran a finger through his hair, tugged at the collar of his shirt, handed the microphone to another boy just like him who was going to introduce me to the public; through the window I watched He Who Is Writing the Novel sitting on the quad: in the end he hadn't come into the auditorium; literary magazine, fuck that, I thought. Then, timidly, he lifted one hand, waving to me. And I didn't like that an albino girl sitting next to me noticed our exchange, our broken intimacy; that she moved her eyebrows in response to his wave.

He Who Is Writing the Novel thanked the audience for their interest, squeezed my hand, cleared his throat on my apartment terrace as the wind whipped the trees that night. Good afternoon,
thank you for coming. He gave the microphone to another just
like him, a boy who is also writing the novel, who also squeezed
me, who thanked the audience, looked out at them, and said: all
of you have come to the presentation of the third edition of the
magazine *Suspensión*, but I have to be honest with you: there is
no magazine, the magazine has ended. The magazine is dead,
because paper is dead vegetal carcasses, and so is literature. The
lights were low now, the perplexed albino features of all those
faces of mine, pressed against the glasses of water and the windows of the auditorium. It was night. The wind came in forcefully from the sea and the curtains of my apartment were out of
control. He Who Is Writing the Novel took my face between his
hands, kissed me, and said that he wanted to sleep with me, that
he wanted my body; I kicked him in the ankle and he let me go.
He Who Is Writing the Novel proclaimed the existence of Corporalism; the multitude moved furiously from the university to
the street, one boy wanted to hit him, from all directions people
called him a pretentious asshole, the Breton of porn, a man tried
to grab me around the waist, another took my hand and wouldn't
let go. One went so far as to follow me home. First they threw a
beer bottle from the back of the room, then came the shattering
of wine glasses like a storm on the Neutria pier. They called us
ignoramuses, intellectuals, imbeciles: that Corporalist mafia just
wants publicity, to attract some big publisher, and indeed after a
few days we received a call from a widely circulated newspaper
that wanted to interview us. The auditorium was silent. Sad, He

Who Is Writing the Novel got to his feet, went to the door of the auditorium, left the university, walked to my house, buzzed the intercom, told me that he wanted to talk about the novel that was keeping him from sleep. I, on the other hand, slept deeply against his chest while he ran his fingertips along the nape of my neck and murmured that I should sleep in peace, that this too is written in the only work of Corporalism.

The novel had fifteen chapters—one per month for one year and the following summer—detailing the actions he would take along the path that led from the writing itself to the founding of Corporalism, from the public declaration of the end of literature to the confusion of character, writing, and author. He Who Is Writing the Novel put both hands on my back and let them slide slowly down. We went to my room; he entered and I stayed in the doorway watching him get into my bed, waiting for the groan of the mattress to stop and transform into a moan, into foam, into the sound of a great deal of water filling an immense space that is the ocean and that comes in through the open window of my apartment in Neutria. The same sound that I can no longer hear through the car horns, the house alarms, the TVs, and the screams of no one: the sound of a dead body that climbs out of bed and settles on top of another dead body, just so, with that nighttime silence so necessary for sleep.

THE NOVEL

Carlos had spent that Sunday at his uncle's place, where the whole family had gotten together for a cookout so they could check out his uncle's new property. The sun was setting by the time he went home. The heat was beginning to descend both in the country and in Santiago, but his bedroom, the living room, and the bathroom were cold like always, far from the summer sun. He closed the door. In the hallway there was a leather suitcase; on top of it, an affectionate note indicating that someone would be by that night to pick it up. The paper was signed by his cosmopolitan cousin Alicia. Carlos left the message where it was, he stood still for a moment, sneezed. He removed a tissue from his pocket and blew his nose. He remembered that he should bundle up or he'd catch a cold, that warning he heard in his mother's voice and also in Elisa's every time they heard him sneeze. He went to his room to grab a sweatshirt. In the living room he turned on the standing lamp so he could find the answering machine. There was a message: someone complaining about her terrible memory, asking him to remind her about a trip they had coming up, and to call her. It was the voice of a woman. Carlos's first impression was that it was Elisa, he recognized that deep sleepy voice she spoke with sometimes, but he had no idea what she could've been referring to: during the last few weeks they'd scarcely exchanged a word, they saw each other once at a mutual friend's birthday party and ended up in bed, drunk. But they didn't converse.

He listened to the message again. Elisa always signed off her messages by leaving her name in order to avoid any confusion, because her voice changed: it was like a shrill little girl's when she was happy, like an adolescent's when she had a bad cold or when she was just waking up, like a very thin piece of glass when she wanted to hide something painful. It wasn't Elisa talking, but it sounded so similar; it was just like Elisa's voice, Alicia had commented after reading the paragraph from his novel in which the protagonist tells a man in a bar everything he knows about the albino girl and describes her voice. That day his cousin told him that his female characters would never speak differently than Elisa, because he never listened to anyone else. Carlos defended himself by saying that was how he preferred it, that all the men have his face, that all the women be slight and distant like his girlfriend. Why lie: in those two-hundred-and-some-odd pages there was no city other than the one in which he lived, no one else walking its streets but the two of them, though they were disguised consecutively as detective, as killer, as writer, as albino girl, as beggar, as old woman. He couldn't keep a paralysis from descending from his head to his hand every day that, ready to move forward on some chapter, he sat down in front of the notebook; this should've been resolved when Elisa denied, with a scornful gesture, that there existed any resemblance between her and the albino girl in his novel. And yet when the protagonist tried to listen to the conversations between that albino girl, the professor, and another man, deducing their words from the movement of their mouths through the window pane, hiding between the trees on the plaza, walking anonymous through the foggy nighttime port, it was the voice of Elisa that he inserted into the discussion instead of the girl. And although he would never hear the albino girl, except her *final moan, which she'd utter bleeding on the floor, the protagonist spent days describing a particular emphasis in Elisa's voice. Carlos was still leaning on the small table by the telephone, attempting to reproduce her pronunciation, without any luck. He dialed the number on the answering machine. Hello, he said, is Violeta there? An old woman, half-asleep, muttered that she wasn't there, that she'd gone traveling. He hung up. He sat on the couch, watching the day slowly break. Maybe his cousin and Violeta were going on a trip together, maybe it was a wrong number and the old woman on the other end of the line had been confused. He stared at the leather suitcase in the hallway: someone would come by that night to pick it up. The telephone was ringing, he froze. Hello, he said when he managed to pick it up. It was the same voice that made him nervous, the only one he heard. What's up, how's everything going, was he busy right then. He exhaled. Elisa asked him why his voice sounded so strange, if she'd woken him, and he responded that he was happy to hear from her, that he wanted to see her.*

THE RECIPIENT

This is the first time I am writing here, at this desk that I've had since I was little and that now, in the light coming through the window, looks different. Getting used to living in a house—even though this is also a studio and the smell of Alicia's paintings impregnates the walls—is also new to me. It's a freedom, when all is said and done, to live with my cousin. I know now what it means to live alone.

Things are happening.

I've been imagining a detective story. It occurred to me that I could write a novel of innumerable pages about a girl who, frightened because a man is apparently following her, contacts a detective to help her. She and the detective become friends, they flirt. He ends up obsessed with her and follows her everywhere. I want to sit down every afternoon, take advantage of the dead hours of summer to write. On one of these afternoons the inspiration comes to me. Until I was twelve years old, I invented fairytales and succeeded in getting all my friends to fall asleep when we camped out in the yard at one of our houses. I think that little

Elisa would love to see me plot something out and then, at first, refuse to show it to her—she loves it when I'm mysterious. That story of the girl who gets stalked by the same guy she is paying to protect her has been coming back to me ever since my cousin told it at our uncle and aunt's country house last Sunday. Elisa won't go to family gatherings with me, she says that my relatives talk too much and she gets tired of them asking about her family, of so many little kids relentlessly running around, crying, shrieking. She says any day now some kid is going to fall in the pool and that no one will notice, my uncles cracking up at their crude double entendres, my aunts talking just to talk, and my grandmother sitting in the center, pretending to listen, like she cares about the grades some grandkid got in school, the clothes someone or other bought, the kind words of some relative's loving girlfriend. At least Alicia was always there in some corner, laughing like the others, but laughing to herself, remembering when we saw ghosts roaming the corridors of that immense mansion in Rancagua, or when an older cousin convinced us that our crazed and sick great-grandmother was locked in the forbidden room, the room on the other side of my uncle and aunt's bedroom. And the enormous trunk hidden away in the cellar, what's in there?, we would ask. That Sunday my cousin Alicia and I talked almost all afternoon. I told her I wanted to live alone that next year and she invited me to come check out her home-studio on Calle Bustamante, she could rent me a room there. And that's where I'm writing this now. She also told me about her friend Violeta. Bored of living in the cesspool of Santiago (my cousin's words), she moved to another city—I can't remember which one—for a couple years. She met a guy there, a classmate at the university, with whom she went out and then broke up. The guy was unhinged and wouldn't leave her alone, calling her on the phone every night, following her through the streets, buzzing the intercom at her apartment and not saying anything when she answered. One day, desperate, it occurred to her to ask a professor friend from the university for help, and he managed to get the guy expelled, but that was worse: one time the guy, furious, almost hit her with his car, and another time he almost pushed her into the city's river. She loved where she was living, but in the end Violeta had to go back to Santiago. What she doesn't know is if the guy followed her here or if she just had the terrible luck of encountering another psychopath. Alicia was very worried when she told me this, her friend is receiving letters that are making her paranoid, lately she thinks she sees that guy on every corner. There aren't many girls like Violeta, according to Alicia, and that's why men go crazy for her. This is a story I'd love to be able to write.

But something's happening. I got home in the afternoon and there was little Elisa, napping on the sofa, a serious expression on her face. I wasn't expecting her, I thought she was going to the beach for the weekend; she'd decided to stay at the last minute, she said. I said great and gave her a quick hug without squeezing her, just the way she likes, and yet she remained silent, indifferent. I gave her a bunch of quick kisses, I sat calmly beside her without touching her, I gave her names (she always likes that): My Little Lady, The Little One, The One with the Waist, The One with Hair in Her Eyes, The One with the Lips. She told me to be quiet. She stood up suddenly and went over to the little table by the phone to pick up some pencil drawings that were sitting there. She had to go, she apologized, she came back to the couch where

I was lying with open arms. She threw a heavy white envelope at my head. I read the name of the sender: Violeta Drago. Elisa asked me what this was all about. Someone had dropped off a letter from this Violeta, who was she and why was she sending me little messages. I asked if she'd seen the person who delivered it, she said no, then I went up to her and smiled calmly, there was no reason to get upset and confuse things. I told her not to be silly, that she was being paranoid: Violeta Drago was just one of my cousin's friends.

Later we drank tea with Alicia and a friend who'd come to visit her. Afterwards we were watching a movie, lying down, and Elisa decided she wanted to spend the night at home, alone, so I took her. I don't know why I'm so tired, and I can't go back to bed either. It's cold inside this house, as if it weren't summer. I know that if I go to sleep, I'll have that same nightmare, the one that won't leave me alone, that nightmare that seems to come with this house: I open my eyes and look out of a curtainless window that turns into the window of an intercity bus. The landscapes pass rapidly before my eyes, the hills expand until they swallow the fields, and the bus begins to descend. Now we are arriving at a port, beyond you can see lights, many lights, and the sea.

◆

November 22nd

(I find myself sitting in class. My eyes, my tongue, my temples will burst if I go on; it's as if I were insisting on leaving behind the here and now of my Latin American Literature class, at 11:45

in the morning, in the second to last seat in the final row on the right-hand side, to transform myself into the guy who complains about his professor, who meets his people, reads his pages, walks in his footsteps, kisses his girl; to transform myself into the girl who's sitting beside me, be made of her long bones, adopt her cautious stride, smell her cleanness on my skin, feel how that black dress falls across my body and how my feet sustain the weight of those enormous boots, to touch with those fingers my nearly nonexistent nose, the way she looks at me now and smiles for no reason yet with beguiling kindness, to see out of her bright eyes, to feel the spring air on my face coming in through the window, to be a woman and respond with a kind expression that I'm unable to describe when people say Alicia. Transform myself into someone else who's watching us from the opposite side of the room, who sees us flirting and imagines that we love each other, that we have loved each other, and that we will love each other right now as she rests her head on my shoulder. To fixate, from the other side of the room, on my imperturbable expression, see that Alicia looks up and notices, for the first time, the movement of my pen across the page, and how her attention shifts to me until her face is transfigured by terror when she reads what I'm writing in this moment: "see that Alicia looks up and notices, for the first time, the movement of my pen across the page, and how her attention shifts to me until her face is transfigured by terror when she reads what I'm writing in this moment: see that Alicia looks up and notices, for the first time, the movement of my pen across the page, and how her attention shifts to me until her face is transfigured by terror when she reads what I'm writing in this moment." I keep writing and she tries to stop me by reading to the end of the paragraph before I get there, when the page is still blank; I battle against this interference and keep on writing while, in the room's other corner, I see that the girl in the last row on the right-hand side is looking anxiously at the notebook of the guy sitting next to her, that she smiles a smile full of mockery and then starts laughing sonorously, the burst of her husky voice interrupting the professor; she starts to read aloud, almost yelling, what it says in the notebook of her classmate, who [the scene is absurd] doesn't seem to notice and keeps on writing. The other students start chuckling when they hear the albino girl read that embarrassing text, the emphasis she puts on certain words, and the guy starts to sweat. Alicia is tearing me apart, the delusion of suspending her movement on this page with my writing turns into simple rambling when my words become public, when what I write is a spectacle for other people who don't know who we are and that this notebook is full of personal things, when they scorn what I say [horror], fixing their ears and filthy eyes on Alicia's chapped lips, which could never utter anything hurtful.

Suddenly the boy, that strange boy who was watching the albino girl with feverish eyes and incessantly taking notes, jumps up from his seat like a hungry animal; with a crack he slams his notebook down on the linoleum and takes off running toward the door. He disappears into the hallway. The professor makes an ironic comment. The albino girl, the only person not laughing, gets up to go to the bathroom; they meet on the quad. He is sitting in the sun, his look is different, it seems to be directed at something very far away, lacking the permanent shadow of worry that had previously marked it. She sits down next to him. They talk for a while, calmly, as if they'd been together for years, as if they were married and they both knew the exact amount of time it took the other to say something. I don't know if they kiss or lean in close to share a secret that no one, absolutely no one else can hear. Then he takes a wallet out of his backpack and from the wallet he removes two bus tickets. She moves her head, we suppose that she's agreeing to go on a trip with him, but where are they going? He asks her what time it is and they get up and walk together down the hallway toward the campus entrance. He looks at everything along the way with tenderness: it's the last time that he'll pass this way, that he'll perceive the aroma of photocopies, the posters promoting parties or offering to share an apartment's rent, the last time he'll hear the phrases of friends greeting each other, the condescending tone of a professor who bumps into a student leaving the bathroom, heading toward the quad of the drama department. I choose to follow the boy and not the girl, in the moment that they separate: he walks down Calle Los Leones, takes the metro of the same name, stares at the faces of the passengers the whole ride, gets off with the majority of them at the Universidad de Santiago station, heads with his backpack toward Terminal Sur. It's not a big deal, I think, he must be going to visit his parents in Rancagua; but he boards a bus whose destination I don't recognize, a bus that surprises me not because of the color of it's paint or because of how few people occupy its seats, but because of the name of its destination: Neutria. I wave to the driver, the engine is already in drive. The baggage handler asks me if I have more luggage, I shake my head.

He glances nervously at his watch. Out the window he recognizes a short girl running in vain to catch the bus, already pulling away from one of the platforms, he tries to remember her name but cannot. He clings to his backpack like a child bound for the unknown as the bus begins to pick up speed. He thinks that right now Alicia is frightened in her room, that she has locked herself in, and is studying the portrait of Violeta or of herself on the beach, with dark sunglasses and a black dress in the middle of summer. He doesn't want to be dead, and yet he's moving toward Neutria. In the seat next to him an unfamiliar woman is sleeping, he looks out the window, I look out the window at the landscape that grows steeper all the time, full of rocks, precipitous, dangerous. Suddenly I see that it's snowing, that snow is falling from the sky and the bus will have to stop.)

THE NOVEL

The doorbell rang. Carlos muted the TV and hurried to turn on lights in his bedroom, the hallway, the living room, and the kitchen, as well as the lamp outside. He was about to turn the knob, just as the doorbell rang for a second time. Elisa was waiting for him, almost falling against the door, with a smile that vanished just as soon as her arms touched his and, instead of greeting her, Carlos asked a question: had she lost her key? She was having trouble speaking, could they please close the curtains and turn off the lights, she said, so that no one would see them from the street. Then, in the armchair, she wrapped her arms around her legs and buried her face between her knees: there was something Elisa didn't want to see, or wished she'd never witnessed, thought Carlos as he went through the house flipping switches. In the kitchen he found a long white candle; he lit it, let a few drops of wax fall in an ashtray, stuck it there, went to the living room, and sat down timidly next to his girlfriend. Outside a strange wind was blowing, it made the windows vibrate. Gently she stretched one arm across his chest, murmuring that tonight there was a full moon. I had another bad dream, she said, like back in high school: she found herself in the faraway south, on the ranch of one of her father's friends, a pampa of such uniformly short grass that, from where she'd materialized, she could see, in the distance, the inhospitable waves *of the Strait of Magellan. The landscape was empty, as if the hundreds of cows, the house, and the garden had been uprooted by a storm. She was running, unable to stop, across the pastures, struggling, soaked by rain, to advance through the mud, she could make out the sea and experienced a feeling akin to hope; then she tripped. She stayed on the ground looking at the palms of her hands and her scraped knees, dirty, bleeding. When she lifted her head and continued to run, she discovered that the hopeful vision of the sea was, suddenly, terrifying. None of her muscles obeyed her. On the shore was a boat that appeared ready to launch, to save itself from the imminent rising of the storm. Or maybe she fell again and saw, in the distance, the boat begin to depart without her. They couldn't wait for her anymore. Before she lost sight of the crew in the shadow of the storm, she was able to make out the silhouette of Carlos, an oar in his hands, his posture severe. Then she ran on, the mud came up to her knees and she was drenched; crying, she fell to the ground again. When she saw the empty sea, she felt calm for a moment, allowing herself to forget the need to reach the shore, until the vessel reappeared in which Carlos and the others made the decision to leave her behind one, ten, a thousand times.*

THE SENDER

What I knew would happen has happened, but the flow of these pages has carried it far away, to the point of transforming it into the irredeemable—the only true word among these I've written to you—into a light that flickers in the distance, like a cruel lighthouse that lures you to the rocks, to collision: my notebook pages have run out, I wrote two words in the empty space beyond the white, on the table. Better still is the image of a lighthouse extinguished in the cloudy Neutrian night; I reminded myself that I'm writing you so that the two of us might see each other before this is over. Imagine a lighthouse abandoned in the night, and you trapped in the darkness of that lighthouse, and me in a boat without oars, adrift.

Me, you, the lighthouse, and the boat occur to me with the certainty that today I am departing, now that Neutria has left me for the last time. You don't realize that the only way to enter this city is to remove it from inside me, liberating that which I invented out of my presence so that anyone at all might inhabit it; the certainty that the end of my life in Neutria is the end of my life strikes me all at once, like a branch being torn free by the wind and falling on the roof of this house. How foolish I was to flee from the city of my childhood so that He Who Is Writing the Novel wouldn't follow me, as if it were possible for one to choose between soul and body, as if staying alive depended on keeping the body far away from the gunshots and the blades, though my soul—just like there exist abandoned boats, floating at high sea—has stayed in Neutria and this body continues writing to you in Santiago. Finding myself in my grandmother's house—when you rang the doorbell and laughably pretended to be someone else, someone named Carlos, and called me The Little One—I became aware that you wanted to enter Neutria through me, but I didn't let you. You wanted to make your soul enter my body and, because this is impossible except through writing, I wrote you one, two, three novels in order to please you. I'm leaving them here for you, on this table in an envelope—if you dare to take it when you come—where between simulacra you will see that you are in fact entering an other: yourself. And because we die we have no body; it's another deception of those who've studied everything, of your friend the professor, who even planned that I should write this last letter.

What terrifies me is that if you don't come to take me, I'll have to go alone, that if that happens this letter will be my last useless act. I move through the house like a thirsty animal that stumbles while carrying cups of water and spills them; the water runs across the parquet floor and is nevertheless absorbed by a dry earth that calls to me. This is vengeance. When finally you enter Neutria, when you are living there and you don't know just what it is that bothers you in that longed-for place, it will be me. In the names of the streets, in the letter you receive, in the darkness of your bedroom my remnants will resound. But I must speak quick and clear, because in my grandmother's trunk I've only discovered fifteen old sheets, like fifteen opportunities to remain blank, yellowing, ancient, that are wasted once covered with ink.

You and those identical to you who make up the Corporalist group had delineated a plan that would end with your disappearance, like what happened to The Young Poet. According to the plan that you'd written in your novel you were going to submit yourself, step-by-step, to various humiliations, wrapping pages of *Canto General* around rocks and throwing them through the windows of the Neutrian Writers' Society. You'd be detained, taken away, and, while being tortured, recite paragraphs from Walt Whitman. The professor would get you out so that by the afternoon you'd already be covering the walls of the Neutria municipal theater with cheap professions from *Corporalization Manifesto*; the next day that supposedly secret text was reproduced in all the newspapers alongside a photo of you tattooing a Marinetti verse across your whole chest. You screamed in pain in downtown Neutria, because you'd cut your arms with razor blades, smearing shop windows with blood—that's what the novel ordered you to do that day—and you were arrested again for disturbing the peace. In jail you were raped by four prisoners, because you punched one of them when he laughed at you; you said nothing, you did not waver at all when confronted with the demands of each phase of the plan: bottles broken over your head during a fight in a Lárico poets' bar, twenty-one days drinking only wine, bathing naked in the fountain in the Plaza de Armas wearing nothing but a heavy mask of Enrique Lihn. How you let a little boy who assaulted you on a corner of the most dangerous shantytown in the port stab you, the tears on your face as he buried the blade in your shoulder. You were accused so many times of inciting violence, at the stadium you went into the bar wearing the rival jersey, whistling every time one of the local strikers got near the goal. They accused you of being deranged, of being an imbecile, they said you were a mental patient: on TV a senator offered to have you interned at an asylum on his dime; a journalist used you as an example of compromise and rebellion in a magazine, later you spit on his hands in a press conference. You regretted none of it, because each one of your misdeeds were systematically announced in your paragraphs, and a boy just like you was following you everywhere to write down a detailed chronicle of your actions in his notebook, another novel that would be the register of the long, sweaty workdays of Corporalism. One hand on my waist, the other on a recording device, the third scratching a wall, and the fourth writing the novel of the novel; in this way we passed the time together, because when He Who Is Writing the Novel ceased to appear, the movement would end, so it was possible to read the manifesto in your notes: the written register of your body's transition—from a clean and fresh body, to a filthy, wrinkled body, torn to its furthest reaches by hairs, scars, hematomas, scratches, marks, irritations, encrusted metals, bleedings, pusses, and gangrenes—was proof that body and literature are incomplete words; how then to speak of the soul, of permanence? I was watching how you doused yourself with gasoline, lit a match, wrote something down about the man in flames, asking me how I could love you, what the name of this thing that united us was, what place you occupied in the painting of Neutria that I was finally describing in my pages. Then you took my hand and told me to be calm, that in the novel a woman appeared walking on the beach, looking somberly at the sea, and it was me—little because you saw me from far away—the albino girl, who would carry out a culminating role in the History of Corporalism.

As if at the same time we were somewhere else, He Who Is Writing the Novel accompanied me every morning to the beach. We walked across the sand holding hands, we stopped to kiss each other, we fell down together and then I had to get up, to keep going, while He Who Is Writing the Novel stayed on the sand, watching me. Sometimes I thought I noticed that a man just like him was filming us from a distance while we rolled around together, and simultaneously I kept walking toward the sea with my notebook, while at my side you asked me why we weren't going to my apartment. I held your hand in silence, how insistent you were. Sitting in the sand I dedicated myself to the painting of the beach of Neutria; the rolling wave in its coming and going, frustrated by the tide that rose as the sun shifted position in the sky, the water insisted on continuing to be the word water, it made me want to throw my notebook as far as I could to see how the sea sank any attempt to immobilize it, and I kicked you, and shouted: imbecile, can't you see I want permanence, and you just the opposite, you want disappearance. You're going to kill me. You laughed at my cries while napping on the sand; you hadn't slept much that week because you stayed up every night writing the novel. But that was impossible, we members of Corporalism knew that after He Who Is Writing the Novel marked the final period nobody would be able to change even a comma of the plan. Right then you confessed that you were going to change the novel's ending, that every night you reread the chapters so that it wasn't the protagonist who died, while during the day you kept on pretending that your body was irredeemably destroying itself. Another wave broke, a boy built a sand castle near where we held each other. During the day you tried to rape a schoolgirl in some Neutrian plaza, in full view of everyone so that they'd lynch you, yet at night you make corrections: as he was spreading the girl's legs he saw in her face the woman he loved. The scream was her scream, the pain was her pain. So night after night, chapter after chapter, Corporalism passed from a manifesto about death to a love story, you told me, and without writing anything new, every night you asked the same question: how to tell the untellable. I embraced you, happy: from a love story to a novel about the salvation of a character. I always forgave your pretentiousness. I loved you so much. And we stayed there, lying on the sand, holding each other. The waves retreated, the sun set, you left, I stayed there describing how the tide went out in my picture. The lighthouse of Neutria was already lit. Suddenly someone identical to you sat down next to me and took my hand in the darkness. He Who Is Writing the Novel squeezed my fingers forcefully, he kissed me all over and even bit me, and in the end he threatened me so I'd stop writing Corporalism in my way: I am just a useful narrator here, and if the character takes the novel too far, the author might find himself forced to make her die.

In the darkness of the beach, I seemed to also see that a pale girl was attentively watching me and He Who Is Writing the Novel— the couple that we formed for a second, holding hands, while he threatened me—observing us and taking notes; a girl like me, who went to my spot, who walked the streets of Neutria with me, who arrived at the entrance to my building, went up in the elevator, took out the key, entered my room, felt the need to take off her clothes, went to the bathroom, splashed water on her face and albino hair. In the dining room she found a note from her friend Alicia that said: I'm sick of this place, I'm going back to Santiago. The girl put her clothes back on, and took a taxi to the Neutria bus station. On the way she noticed that the streetlamps were falling from their posts, cars were entering a nonexistent roundabout, people were going into unnumbered houses, kids on bicycles in the plaza were turning where there wasn't a corner, the trees were growing, dense, becoming a forest, exuberant vegetation untouched by human beings. Instead of a city there appeared a small village, then a military stronghold, four Spaniards dismounting and building a fire on which to cook, three natives chasing two animals leaving an egg hidden in a cave that is nothing but dry earth, dust, gas, emptiness.

A hand rose to wave goodbye to the albino girl at the entrance to the bus station and it was her own hand; no, it was the hand of the taxi driver who was touching her shoulder, asking if she was feeling okay. She didn't trust him, she paid and ran to the entrance, fearful that the ground on which she walked would cease to exist before she could find the bus. She remembered her dear Alicia, she half turned to look for her and in that instant a girl emerged out of her own back, took two steps, dropped an empty cup in a trash can, climbed onto the first step of the bus that in eight hours would drop me off in Santiago. For a long time, I was afraid. I lay down in my bedroom, alone, wondering why I'd let Alicia leave Neutria without saying goodbye. Every now and then my grandmother poked her head in to offer me lunch, tea, cookies; she asked me if I was feeling okay, she stroked my face with one hand that, before settling on my forehead, she waved from side to side as if she were saying goodbye to me. According to my grandmother—who actually died when I was eight—I was shaking with fever, delirious, saying that you were coming to find me at my apartment, that I couldn't understand how the city remained standing if I wasn't observing it, if I wasn't able to make the waves break at my feet on the beach, if from my bed here in Santiago all I see is Cerro San Cristóbal. I slept with my grandmother's hand on my forehead—now and then I saw her move her head with the sort of swaying acquired by everything that drifts away—sweating and shouting where had He Who Is Writing the Novel gone, if he'd forgotten me because my sick body would be of no more use to him, unable to escape my nightmare: I walked for days through the city, I was unable to lift my head to see where I'd come to. Until I woke up. Soaked with sweat, I went to the bathroom and looked at myself in the mirror: out the window was the university, the port, and beyond that, the sea. I understood that if Neutria was still standing it was because you and I met each other, because I told you that dying isn't necessary and you answered with a proposition: better that we live together. I took off my pajamas, showered, got dressed again. On the answering machine I had a message from the professor, who invited me to the opening of an art show that he'd organized in the exhibition hall at Universidad de Neutria.

The sun was setting again. The streetlamps barely cast any light, as if they were coming to understand that the city was slowly entering the night and would never return. As I went turning down the corridors on my way to the university auditorium, I heard a deep voice that unexpectedly narrated in detail, through some speakers, every step I was taking: she passes through the grayish gateway into the dark space of the central nave, passes through another archway down a new, still-darker corridor. She arrives at the central quad, turns—furious, sad, beside herself— to the left to enter the exposition hall. From a dais, dressed in meticulous mourning, smiling, the professor lifted his left hand and waved to her, leaving the microphone for a moment, no longer narrating my footsteps, because I took three glasses of wine and clutched them against the palms of my hands before hurling them against the dais, where he was now commenting to other academics about my gesture, about memory, about the social body, about collective intimacy, about private horizons. I hurled the glasses against the wall behind the fucking professor, I broke into pieces, and the red stained the whiteness of the wall at least.

The guests at the opening of the *Corporalism* show, the most recent work of documentary fiction by the famous professor, gathered around the sequence of photos hung in the hall. The first ones depicted girls like me and boys like He Who Is Writing the Novel in a living room, heatedly arguing about A Young Poet who never existed. In the photos that followed we made a toast with whiskey, the three of us, including the artist responsible for the show. This man is a genius, said the Undersecretary of Culture, and studied with interest the huge photo of He Who Is Writing the Novel slicing his index finger on the golden edge of an opulent edition of *Madame Bovary*, whose bloody pages were displayed in the Objects section. Dozens of photos documenting a student march, students who also received cash payment, whose posters proclaimed "Corporalism is fascism," the stones thrown at the Biblioteca Nacional, the frustrated arson attempts at the houses of Eltit, Richard, and Zurita; hundreds of photos that established the chronology of the "Birth," "Adolescence," and "Death of an artistic movement." Across one wall was printed the *Corporalization Manifesto*, at last I was able to read what you'd written in order to make me understand that a great artifice was making it so the wine glasses kept falling all around me without hurting me, so the light bulbs shattered without their brightness leaving me blind, otherwise I'd have been unable to witness the exposition of every single one of these words, of every blink of my eyes, of my name itself which had been foreseen by that professor: while He Who Is Writing the Novel and I were creating it, someone else was gathering together our pages like the corpus of an academic essay that would bear the title *Loquela*.

When another wine glass fell to the floor of the exhibition hall, I drew near to see if it had actually broken, and I heard the long-winded speech the professor was delivering to an art critic: with this installation I explore the emotional emptiness of individuals as the foundation of a society of consumption that conceives of itself as a healthy organism, where the artist is paradoxically the cancerous tumor and the only individual without needs; the economic order is maintained by a structure that is doubly hypocritical with respect to cultural creation, since as much as this system of exchange convinces the artist of the uselessness of his work, it demands that his face, his name, and his body be a polemic object in a scenario of psychological degradation and social marginalization where anyone can read the limitations of the market without experiencing them personally, or simply to conceive of marketing campaigns that seek the socialization of consumption. Corporalism—declared the professor in words that wanted to break against me and stain the white wall of this house from where I write you—is the dramatization of all the errors we artists commit, most of the time due to ingenuousness, alcoholism, or ambition, until we turn our own bodies into metastasis. Instead of spilling what is imposed on us across a page and giving it back in the form of book, instead of offering society that tumor, which is why they pay us to study in their laboratories, we mix ourselves into the work itself and end up presenting our bodies in pieces on silver platters so that the attendants of openings and launches can devour us. I divined what the professor wanted to add and he was quiet: the artist is a tumor that should not spread, but that must exist to focus the malignance. He believed himself to be an artist, because of that he was the most despicable being on Earth, I thought when I came to the photograph in sepia where you and I are holding each other on the beach; you were biting my ear and I was slipping my hand into your pants, we were standing and the sea was a monochrome wall of water. It had stopped moving at last! That was the photo, the picture I'd been seeking for so long across the eternity of a couple: the missing landscape that kept Neutria from leaving me, the last photo in the final room of the show.

On my shoulder I felt the weight of a hand that slid down to my waist, a warm hand that was cooling against my flesh and grabbing me. I turned: He Who Is Writing the Novel was in front of me, dressed elegantly, hair gelled and slicked back like an executive. He smiled at me with malice; I asked him if he was happy with the way his novel had ended—a huge party, fame and posterity in the media. Without blinking he said that I could stick posterity wherever it fit, that he didn't want to talk: I had to leave with him. He tried to drag me and I put up a fight, threatening to scream. He said that the others like him, who are writing the novel of Corporalism and who were wandering around the exhibit, wouldn't let me off the hook if they saw me again. I shuddered. My voice breaking, I asked him what he was talking about. He said that I shouldn't pretend like I didn't understand, that the limits of the movement were inside the body of its protagonists, that the end of Corporalism was the end of its characters. I still didn't understand: it had all been staged by the professor and had turned out just how he'd planned. No, that wasn't so, he responded. The implications and phases were much vaster: I would never be able to see the magnitude of all of it, the professor and his exhibit formed part of something greater. Like how the bricklayer does not imagine the dimensions of the city when he builds his first house?, I asked. He looked at me in silence. I had contributed to the failure of this part of the project, he murmured. My presence and the disgusting sentimentalism of He Who Is Writing the Novel, who had been unable to bear seeing me there, holding him on the beach, assuring him that I loved him, that I loved him completely, standing, walking, alive. He Who Is Writing the Novel had at last transformed himself into The Young Poet and disappeared without leaving traces or records. Gently I pulled my arm from the hand that was clutching me. He stayed there sitting on the quad, watching me walk toward the exit; he was unable to keep himself from shouting after me, from a distance: You're going to die.

I'm already coming to the end of my letter, my dear. I write you at the hour of greatest silence in this city that is never silent, at sunrise in this Santiago where the sun never rises. Now the wind off the river comes against the windows of this house, it makes them shake but they remain intact, like writing on paper; it pushes the white of the page, it dirties but doesn't rip it. I hope this happens when I have nothing left to tell you, when the only thing left is the description of the coastline of Neutria vanishing behind me as I dragged my suitcase toward the bus station, running away before He Who Is Writing the Novel appeared with his gun and left me there on the floor, my eyes filled with their own liquids, which would prevent me from seeing how the ocean rose up, sweeping away the beach, the pavement, the avenues, the valley of Neutria, filling the empty space above it with water, the empty space which I'd filled first with little houses, then a pier, businesses, plazas, buildings, schools, a university, a stadium, and a touristic boardwalk along the sea so that people would come from other places to live here, so that a couple who walked through the university entrance would take each other by the hand, decide to love each other, pass time and grow old together, in these streets, weep for the other at his or her funeral; but the water will also sweep away this Neutrian cemetery where I won't end up because it will have died with me, because it isn't possible to put a body in a page, because paper isn't earth.

I tried to drag my suitcase full of notebooks through the trash-cans, the rubble, and the enormous dust cloud: with each passing step the cement threatened to cease covering the ground. When I came to the Black River I saw that the bridge had surrendered to the erosion, so I had to carefully descend the damp hillside where I sank into mud up to my knees. It wouldn't be easy to get away from you that way; nor was I able to run when I saw the beggars who sleep under the bridge approaching. In the mud-marred landscape I distinguished their shaved heads, the firebrands on their naked skins, their faces painted with lime—the last vestiges of the most recent raid by the city's sanitary services—that surrounded me and touched me, emitting hoarse moans, pulling at my clothes with hands covered in sores, tearing them. Beggars emerged from ruins across the city, all of them wanting a piece of me: they appeared in multitudes on the street, limping as they forded the river that no longer existed, barely splashing me at all with its remaining puddles, tugging at my skin through mutterings that were senseless yet rhymed nonetheless. As they spread my legs they incessantly asked a question that only my pain could answer. When I was able to stand and tried to run, I understood what one of them was saying: I was The Young Poet, I wanted to throw myself into the river, but a beggar caught me, threw me harshly to the ground, got on top of me and screamed that he was The Young Poet; another limping beggar approached, another, and many more who surrounded me, threw me down again and got on top of me, howling the same sentences: I was The Young Poet, I wanted to throw myself into the river, but a beggar caught me, threw me harshly to the ground, got on top of me and screamed that he was The Young Poet; another limping beggar approached, another, and many more who surrounded me, threw me down again and got on top of me, howling the same sentences: I was The Young Poet, I wanted to throw myself into the river, but a beggar caught me, threw me harshly to the ground, got on top of me and screamed that he was The Young Poet; another limping beggar approached, another, and many more who surrounded me, threw me down again and got on top of me, howling the same sentences. I ran and ran and ran through the mud, escaping. Until the sun came up.

A man found me walking with lost eyes. He climbed over the bridge rail, slipped through the bars, down to the river bed, took my arm, put his jacket around my shoulders to keep me warm, got me out onto the street, asked me what I was doing down there in the disgusting Mapocho, and so early. He told me he was going to take me to the house; the house, he said. That made me mistrustful. When I asked his name, he responded with a grimace. Before you could pull out your gun, I forced myself to run again, and lost you at a stoplight. All the way home. My grandmother, who was eating breakfast, rebuked me for getting home at such an hour and in such a state; she called me a whore. I agreed, agreed so much that I started to cry. Finally I went to my room and fell asleep.

In the afternoon my grandmother had gone out. You appeared again; you wouldn't leave me alone. This time you pretended you were a friend of the family, that you were passing through the neighborhood and you wanted to stop in for a visit, you shyly introduced yourself as someone else, with a name that made me laugh. You claimed not to know me, but went to get in bed with me anyway; I made you believe we were going to sleep together. And for the first time. Then Alicia called on the phone to invite me to her birthday. You can't miss it, she said. You asked me who was calling, I responded no one important. I thought I was lying to you, yet immediately I knew it was true, because Alicia could no longer do anything for me. You found me, there's no way out. The sound of a current of air, across the metal of the hinge, I feel the wind of the river on my face: someone is opening the door. I'm waiting for you now, I'm going to stop writing so you can come in.

Oh God.

THE NOVEL

Elisa said she'd wondered why Violeta was just sitting there. Like she was waiting for her, Elisa saw a space between two cars and parked immediately, not thinking about what she was doing and not hearing the instructions of the old man with a rag for washing windshields: pull forward just so, turn in a bit more. The old man smiled at her, she ignored him. She took the path through the plaza toward the bench where she'd seen Violeta. The albino girl was holding a notebook in her right hand across her knees, hunched over, tense. Suddenly she shut her eyes and started writing. Elisa watched her from where she was leaning against a tree. She'd never seen a person like her before, such pale skin; when she didn't move for a few seconds, she looked lifeless. No, not like a lizard, Elisa answered. Like a woman made of marble, maybe, she said when they asked her for a description, but she wasn't referring to those actors who dress up as statues, like the detective who was trying to flirt with her had stupidly suggested. For moment it had seemed to her that time had stopped, perhaps because Violeta was writing in her notebook without paying attention to the movement of the pen. Yes, she'd had to look at the clock to realize she didn't care at all about the time. Then she pressed the little black bag against her waist, walked to the bench, and sat down beside her. Breathing heavily, she leaned against the wooden backrest and looked at Violeta out of the corner of her eye: now she was turning the pages one after another, not reading them, as if she were reviewing the appearance of each page, looking for flaws, focusing on the layout of the letters and on the blank spaces, just like she liked to do herself, not reading. Violeta turned her face unexpectedly and asked her if she was Elisa, little Elisa. She didn't know what to do, she pressed her hands against the wood of the seat to take stock of her own body and not feel even smaller in front of that woman, like a little girl beside her older cousin, she said, and tried to ignore the disapproving eyes of the detectives, absorbed in her tits.

She nodded, Violeta had responded by saying she didn't remember having seen her before and yet she recognized her, because Alicia was so precise in her descriptions of people. Elisa didn't like imagining the two of them talking about her at all, about her appearance, about her clothes; nor did she want to know why she came up in their conversations, she told the detective. Anyway, she gave Violeta an angry look, and Violeta sighed deeply, like she'd been crying for days, like a mute person registering a complaint. Only then did she smile; not to enter into confidence or anything like that, but to curtly tell her that, after all, she was the longtime girlfriend of the dearest cousin of her best friend. Elisa hadn't dared to get up and run away, so affected was she by the way Violeta spoke, similar, she thought, to how she felt when her older brothers told horror stories around bonfires in the country so many years ago; after a silence they'd look at her and say, slowly: it was the devil incarnate.

And yet she preferred to tell the detectives that Violeta put the notebook in her backpack indifferently, that they sat there for several minutes without saying anything, until they caught sight of large columns of smoke pouring out of the roof of a bakery on the opposite side of the street. People were growing agitated, an old couple went over to see what was going on, the shopkeepers came curiously out into the street, and a group of children on bicycles went to alert the police at a nearby station. The plaza had emptied out where they were sitting, while on the next block the cars, the crowd, the jets of water, and the flames mixed noisily together. At last, Violeta smiled, for some reason the fire made her laugh. How cruel, how irresponsible, how foolish; that's what Elisa thought then, but she said nothing, instead it was the albino girl who spoke: it's so hot here, all the houses could catch fire. In the end, that was Santiago, hot or cold there was always smoke, so a fire shouldn't be some kind of novelty. In a new silence, contaminated by the firefighters' sirens, Elisa had begun to feel nervous again, recalling another chapter she'd read in Carlos's novel: for several blocks, the protagonist followed the albino girl, who was looking for an address she'd written down on a piece of paper. Suddenly he'd seen her stop, mouth agape, watching how the firefighters were putting out a fire in what was left of a house. The protagonist went a little closer to listen to the discussion the albino girl was having with a captain, who was trying to disperse the onlookers; he told her that if she lived there she would be considered a suspect, since the fire had been intentional. The albino girl laughed in the firefighter's face: think what you like, but this is not my fire. Violeta coughed before interrupting Elisa's thoughts to tell her that she'd read that there exist three types of fire, explosive fires, flaming fires, and smoking fires; she preferred the first ones. From a distance someone was trying to evacuate people with a megaphone, but nobody was moving and the air was growing heavier all the time. Violeta insisted that she hated smoke, then she said that this wasn't her fire. Elisa didn't tell the detectives about any of the coincidences; instead she stated that she'd stared at Violeta and asked what she was writing in her notebook. She wanted to threaten her directly, to get her to stop sending messages to her boyfriend, to have her leave them in peace, but she didn't talk about that either. She was starting to like Violeta and, at the same time, she knew they'd never be friends; she hadn't grown paler in that moment, that was impossible, nor had she blushed, Elisa explained. She had simply answered with a different face: she was writing about a dream she'd had. Elisa didn't know what to say, she felt arrogant, intrusive, uncomfortable. As if all the weight of the silence of that conversation was on top of her, without pausing she said the first thing that came into her head: many of her friends had dream notebooks and all of them would rather burn those pages than let anyone see them, except for the pages they were forced to write for their psychologist. The wail of a siren interrupted her. The firefighters tried in vain to disperse the crowd, hypnotized by the flames that were swallowing the roof of the bakery. Violeta covered her ears. Elisa did the same. When calm returned, the albino girl put her hand on the zipper of her backpack and said in a low voice that she had the same dream every night, though the faces and names of those vile men changed. The smoke lowered across the plaza. The albino girl smiled at Elisa, coughed, stood up, and walked away. She never saw her again, she assured the detective. Later on she'd swear that Carlos's novel, which they discovered in Violeta's house, had never left her hands.

THE RECIPIENT

December 9ᵗʰ

From here onward the only excision will consist in referring to you with just the initial of your first name. I'm sitting at the base of a tree in the Plaza de Armas, I'm not in Neutria and it seems like I won't ever be; I lift my head and can see perhaps the only peaceful space in this city of shrieking and taunting: the façade of the cathedral, lit from below. The severe, illuminated statue of the carpenter Joseph, I guess, and above it a glimmering point, the only star in the blind night of Santiago, a night of walls and ceilings in which I'm trapped. The plaza, the new old Plaza de Armas is the only place where I feel alone, where I can be a stranger and weep with my hand covering my face, hearing the songs of the fanatics who preach about the coming inferno, that inferno is already here; the only place I can weep in silence with eyes closed, while people crowd together in order to laugh loudly at two clowns who are also shrieking horrors in the pedestrian walkway, where I can sit down and weep after having walked for several hours, trying to find a miserable church and its silence. If I'd been able to come before God in the penultimate pew, face to the floor, asking why

I have to lose you, why it's permitted, asking for an answer with the cynicism of knowing that I only ask so that you'll come back, that I want to believe that God exists and there are places that do make sense, where you'll always be waiting for me.

Like an act of honesty and a rupture of the vice of the lie, of obliqueness, that has allowed me to tolerate the great shame of living in this time and in this city of pure death, of beggars, of children coming to hospitals for the beatings and violations of their parents, while we close our eyes so as not to disturb the clean and kind home we're creating on the page; to escape from this vice of creating fictions that aren't as disgustingly transitory as the streets of Santiago, as the gaze of the residents of Santiago, as my writing is filthy; to stop being the writer who doesn't let the clamor and stench enter his room—because you can't work like that—who doesn't let the senselessness of his protagonist touch him in any word, because his work is to write, transcendence be damned; for that I'll sacrifice the narrative perfection of my novel. You know that I'd thought of closing the puzzle with the story that occurred in Neutria, with the past, with the explanation of who was going to kill whom, when, and why. No. Once I told C that I was going to make my novel out of the days, out of what the facts wrote for me. Well, here I am. Trembling because I'm alone after having wept when I discovered that I will not have you if not in transcendence. Pounding on the doors of churches that are closed at this hour of the night. I love you so much and I leave you until next time, until the end of a novel that I thought was worthwhile because in it I was going to save you. I'll write you every day, whenever I can, these letters, until we are together again, wherever it may be; nothing will matter to me, I'll pay no attention to any character, to any action. Objects will cease to be named so that around me everything will begin to disappear, so that the limits of the place where we live might be believable. I'll stop being a voice, I'll be me, I want to go back to speaking sentences and have you by my side, kissing me, telling me what to say.

◆

December 24th

To save you would be beautiful if I could go where I'm going without having to leave the place where I've been. I recite your return letter from memory; you felt me naked against your naked back and I love you. With you I am part of something more, flesh that isn't flesh that will cool but is part of a heartbeat; yours that I hear quicken, your ear on my chest, a movement that traverses everything and includes us when our pulses beat as one, your tongue in mine; you give where you receive, a slap, my fingers hurt and yet it is your fingers that burn against my skin, you remove them and the skin is left bloodless, white, burning, painful. The body is one; a man who is a woman looks to the heavens and between two moans hears the never-still silence of God's contemplation as I want to imagine it; you are the one I could enter without leaving myself. In that moment I looked up and you didn't even tell me that you understood, instead you just stretched out your hand from below to open my eyelids. To save you and together we'd write the end of the novel.

THE NOVEL

Someone would be coming by to pick up the suitcase, Carlos said. Elisa held him tighter, resting her head against his chest. Without listening to him she murmured that it felt like winter, a rainy winter. Carlos ran his fingers through her hair and asked who'd be coming by to pick up the suitcase. She continued, saying that it was like they'd cut off the electricity to all of Santiago and it was only going to come back on after a downpour of many days; only the rubble would be illuminated, wet under the light of a sun that would come out at last. Carlos kissed her. She added that there was no way she was going to answer the phone if it rang again, and he noticed that, in the half-light of the living room, the streetlamp caused a luminous line to come in through a crack between the curtains, falling transversally across the two of them, across the sofa, the glass of the table, and the chair where the suitcase rested. The light divided the living room in half, that space where the two of them took refuge, Elisa said. They continued holding each other in silence, then she began to fantasize that she was interrogating him: she put her chin on her boyfriend's abdomen, face down, so that the questions she asked tickled him and he was unable to answer. Where had her female friends gone, they didn't call her anymore. Why was she so afraid recently, even when they were holding each other; surely she was watching too many movies, reading many books, paying excessive attention to news about wars, assaults, domestic violence, and accidents. When she was asleep she'd wake up because the disc she'd been listening to ended, and at an hour when there wasn't even the sound of cars in the street. She started to tremble. Carlos twisted the hair on the nape of her neck around his fingers and told her to be quiet, sshh, but she asked again why it was so cold if it was summer, and what . . . where did that bell they heard on Sunday mornings come from, if the one time she woke up, got dressed, and went to the church to see, of course, it'd been locked. All the while, he couldn't stop thinking about what he'd done the previous afternoon: he decided to get rid of the notebook containing the detective novel. He'd reviewed the whole thing in a couple of hours, and he was so annoyed by the silence in which he was reading that he ended up saying the dialogues between the protagonist and the other characters out loud, almost shouting; people passing by in the street looked in the window. Sweating, he'd let himself collapse on top of the desk when he realized that there was nothing at all intriguing about a guy who plotted a murder—of the albino girl and of the reader—behind the protagonist's back, it was nothing more than the account of a storyteller obsessed with loneliness, in which there was no room for any characters besides himself. The tale of a suicide that was never named, that's what he'd written; so where did the gunshot and the twisted face in the mirror go? Now he heard Elisa asking why, while napping, she'd had that nightmare: she was a man stranded on a faraway island, she spent innumerable days building a hut and, after she placed the final branch, she went inside to rest; but the structure collapsed and her body was trapped. No, Carlos decided, I'm not going to keep writing the diary of a madman. The first thing to do was tear out the pages of the final chapter; from there he would make a new novel, one in which a man, after an inexplicable tragedy, would find a wife, a family, and a place in the city. He went down to the corner store. This time he picked out a spiral notebook, with three sections and a plastic cover, totally different from the one with sixty yellow pages that he'd found forgotten in his sister's drawer, adorned with only a couple childish drawings on the back cover. Elisa had spoken to him once about a box where she kept things she didn't want to see again but didn't dare throw away. They'd argued about that, and he got the impression that the poems and stories he'd given her in high school were in there, he swore to her that he'd never regret anything he'd written. Okay then, this was the moment to decide, to hide away the voice of that protagonist somewhere that would drown out his cries. Back in the store he found an elegant box that, according to the saleswoman, had once been used to store top hats. He threw the notebook inside, went on foot to the bridge at Pio Nono and Santa María. When he lit the box on fire, the wind unexpectedly ripped it from his hands and hurled it into the Rio Mapocho, for a long time he stayed there, watching how the current carried away the soaked remnants. The stench of the riverbank was nauseating: this was revulsion now, not fear, and he felt relieved. From a payphone he called Elisa and awkwardly told her that he'd burned the story of the albino girl. Elisa interrupted him: coincidently, her clothes smelled like smoke; she'd spent the afternoon talking with Violeta, while the bakery across the street from her house burned. He was silent. The truth, she went on, was that she hadn't told her anything about the letter she'd kept hidden for months now. She couldn't take it anymore, she was going to take it to her now, she would return it and he could do whatever he wanted with the albino girl and her messages. Now Carlos stared into darkness of the living room and kept touching Elisa's soft neck, entranced by the line of light that was falling across the rug as her voice grew almost inaudible, asking why everything creaked in this house, when were they going to bed, why was *she so alone if she wasn't alone. The next day he would personally return Violeta's letter; moreover, he decided, he wasn't going to open the envelope. For him it was enough that he was there, holding Elisa, the two of them sleeping together on the sofa. He was also confident that it was too late now for anyone to come pick up the suitcase, that the next morning the two of them would wake up with the sun on their faces and they'd still be in the same position.*

CORPORALIZATION MANIFESTO

(Unprintable text)

I'll only be satisfied when I sit down to write: I'll find people who share my ideas or whom I'll convince to agree with me. Then I'll try to form a group with them, stating at the outset that the results will depend exclusively on the plurality of the project.

The reader lives and the author has died, we'll proclaim, though our goal will be to resuscitate him, to give him what he never had: body, flesh, presence. And what will die instead is the text, the artistic product that escapes from our hands and becomes merchandise: all the time we spent spilling our blood across the page is transformed into food for publishers, newspapers, critics. That's why we're anemic, that's why we need to suck up the humors of others and end up dissolved in foreign books, that's why we die every time we read, in handwriting that is not our own, a sentence that belongs to us.

We ourselves will be the project, our own breathing will be that of every character we create. The autonomous world of the text will no longer be able to justify this or that coward, because it won't exist anywhere but in each moment of our existence. Every time that a respectable voice pejoratively describes the initial action of one of our chapters, for example, it will be passing judgment on our way of life, which naturally will provoke a reaction. Literature is a fight to the death but, since we are the creators and all the others just have fun at our expense, the balance is leaning in our favor from the beginning. As the virtuosos of the world join Corporalism, the indolent will wonder desperately what inexplicable phenomenon has caused the people to cease, suddenly and en masse, producing works of art. And we'll respond with the joyful silence of those who share a secret.

The reader won't know that we're always finishing a creation, at every moment and according to a composite plan prefigured in advance; he'll only be able to learn of this creation in the records, documents, and expositions charged with making it known that it's time to unveil the word *end*. In any event, we'll take the comments, mutterings, and applause without a care, because to read is to be in the presence of a corpse. We, on the other hand, the ones who survive, find ourselves again at the beginning of the one and only pleasure: we will be fruitful.

THE NOVEL

Carlos was sitting on the sidewalk looking at the ground when Elisa came up in front of him. A patrol car had picked her up around four in the afternoon, they'd asked via the intercom for her to accompany them, because her boyfriend was in trouble. No one said a word to her on the way. Once they got out of the car and entered the cordoned-off area someone spoke to her: there had been a homicide. She froze. Horns sounded in the surrounding streets, a car radio transmitted at full volume a metallic voice that tirelessly insulted someone of an indistinguishable name, while men in uniforms ran from one side to the other and threw crumpled-up pages into the street. The door to an ambulance opened to the rhythm of a piercing alarm, out of it emerged men with gloves, masks, and bags, dozens of bags in their hands.

An officer approached her, muttering that a young man had shot a girl point-blank; he asked her to identify them. She was taken inside a patrol car, where they showed her two photos in which Violeta appeared sitting on a beach, dressed in black, her eyes lost in the ocean. They asked if she knew her: yes, she had spoken to her once. But it appears that your boyfriend knew her better, added the same detective who'd told her first how Carlos had notified them that Violeta was dead, just inside the door of her own house. Elisa paled. Her boyfriend's explanations weren't

sufficient, and now he was detained as a preventative measure, they
informed her. Leaning against the car door, she brought her hand to her
head; she felt like it was nighttime in a foreign town, that an unknown
man was insisting on sharing a motel room with her, that although he
spoke an unfamiliar language she understood him, and yet was unable
to find the expression to reject him. She opened her eyes, she felt a little
dizzy when she asked to see him. That's what she said: take me to him,
let me talk to him.

Carlos was gaunt, the white T-shirt he was wearing was stained with
dirt, his pants too. Elisa asked him, with a knot in her throat, why he
was dirty like that. He stood up, made as if to hug her but two officers
twisted one of his arms so he was rendered immobile. Don't imagine
anything, he told Elisa, almost shouting. He hadn't killed anyone, he'd
just gone out that morning to return Violeta's letter. He rang the doorbell
but nobody answered. He realized that he'd been a fool to go in through
the unlocked gate. His idea had been to slip the letter under the door
but, as soon as he leaned against it, it opened without resistance. Inside
the curtains were drawn, so he took a few steps before tripping over a
shape on the floor. A body covered in blood. And he didn't know it was
a corpse, he told Elisa, like he was talking to the officers. She came close
and took his hand, which had started to tremble in the moment that he
asked her again not to imagine anything, when he told her that everyone
was confused and they all needed someone to blame.

Carlos Labbé, one of *Granta*'s "Best Young Spanish-Language Novelists," was born in Chile and is the author of five novels—including *Navidad & Matanza*, also available from Open Letter—and a collection of short stories. In addition to his writings, he is a musician and has released four albums. He is a co-editor at Sangría, a publishing house based in Santiago and Brooklyn. He also writes literary essays, the most notable ones on Juan Carlos Onetti, Diamela Eltit, and Roberto Bolaño.

Will Vanderhyden is a translator of Spanish and Latin American fiction. He graduated from the MALTS (Master of Arts in Literary Translation Studies) program at the University of Rochester. In addition to Carlos Labbé, he has translated fiction by Edgardo Cozarinsky, Alfredo Bryce Echenique, Juan Marsé, Rafael Sánchez Ferlosio, and Elvio Gandolfo.

Open Letter—the University of Rochester's nonprofit, literary translation press—is one of only a handful of publishing houses dedicated to increasing access to world literature for English readers. Publishing ten titles in translation each year, Open Letter searches for works that are extraordinary and influential, works that we hope will become the classics of tomorrow.

Making world literature available in English is crucial to opening our cultural borders, and its availability plays a vital role in maintaining a healthy and vibrant book culture. Open Letter strives to cultivate an audience for these works by helping readers discover imaginative, stunning works of fiction and poetry, and by creating a constellation of international writing that is engaging, stimulating, and enduring.

Current and forthcoming titles from Open Letter include works from Bulgaria, Catalonia, China, Iceland, Israel, Latvia, Poland, Spain, South Africa, and many other countries.

www.openletterbooks.org